Kiss M... on
the Inside

Kiss Me on the Inside

Janice Burkett

www.urbanbooks.net

Urban Books, LLC
97 N18th Street
Wyandanch, NY 11798

ISBN 13: 978-1-60162-594-6
ISBN 10: 1-60162-594-4

First Printing January 2014
Printed in the United States of America

10 9 8 7 6 5 4 3 2 1

Distributed by Kensington Publishing Corp.
Submit Wholesale Orders to:
Kensington Publishing Corp.
C/O Penguin Group (USA) Inc.
Attention: Order Processing
405 Murray Hill Parkway
East Rutherford, NJ 07073-2316
Phone: 1-800-526-0275
Fax: 1-800-227-9604

Chapter 1

Bzzz, bzzz, bzzz. The battery-powered strap-on vibrated between Keisha's thighs. "Mmmh." Keisha expresses her pleasure as Martin went deeper in her candy pot.

"I know you love it," Martin said with confidence. He didn't have a problem with wearing a strap-on because he knew his manhood was below average length. He had no shame in his game when it came to satisfying Keisha. "Tell me you love it."

Keisha wanted to laugh when the words escaped his lips. But he had touched her spot and her pleasure intensified. "Yes!" Her voice sang. Martin grabbed her thighs, bringing her to the edge of the bed, bringing the sheet with her. The pillow-top mattress gave extra cushion to her back. It felt as if she was sexing on clouds. Martin was working the strap-on like he owned it. "Yes. Yes." Keisha expressed her satisfaction.

"Not yet, baby." Martin stopped her. "I want you to really explode." Martin planted his face between her legs, tasting her flavor.

"Oh! Yessss! Yesss!" Keisha was singing opera.

Keisha's bedroom door flew open, banging into the wall. Martin's tongue was buried deep inside Keisha's love pot. The door being flung open didn't bother him at all.

"Martin!" a woman's voice called out.

Martin picked his head up only to see his wife. Keisha didn't even scream at the intruder; instead, she wore a devious smile as she covered her naked body.

"You damn bastard!" The woman charged inside as if she were a linebacker ready to make a tackle. Martin jumped to his feet and his wife froze seeing the third leg at his knee. Her eyes zoomed in on the strap-on. Keisha had a big smile on her face as Martin tried to use both of his hands to cover his borrowed dick.

He never did anything kinky or freaky with his wife because she was too conservative. He would try to taste her wetness but she would close her legs like a shy schoolgirl and scold him. "Martin, you are a man of God. You should know that's ungodly," she would say. The missionary position was all he was entitled to. But as long as he kept giving Keisha all the shopping sprees and kept fattening her bank account, he could eat from Keisha's cookie jar whenever he wanted.

"Satan! The Lord shall rebuke you!" The woman ran out the door, unable to fathom seeing her husband standing in front of her, marinating in another woman's juice. Martin hopped into his pants, not bothering to take the strap-on off.

"You can keep the dick!" Keisha busted out in a wicked laugh and dropped herself backward on the bed. Her cell phone vibrated on the nightstand and she reached over and picked it up. Still lying on her back she viewed the number. Keisha quickly sat up and accepted the call. "Where the hell are you?" Keisha yelled as she shuffled out of bed and reach for her robe, which was hanging from one of the poles of her king-sized canopy bed. She tied the pink terry-cloth string around her waist. Keisha speed-walked to the bathroom and closed the door behind her. A roll of tissue sat on the toilet seat, so she pressed the speaker button and placed the phone on the granite sink to make her hand available to put a roll of Scott tissue on the holder.

"I said I would do it right?" a deep masculine voice calmly stated.

"Five hours ago," she snapped at him.

"Just remember I'm doing you a favor. It's not my damn job." The man's tone went from nonchalant to harsh.

Keisha took the phone off speaker and placed it at her ear as she walked out the bathroom. "Well, consider it a damn job because if you fuck this up, your ass will be fired." She ended her conversation as she passed by the living room, where her roommate, Nikki, sat, surrounded by medical books. Nikki had an inquisitive look on her face as Keisha walked past her. "Mind your damn business," Keisha hissed before Nikki even uttered a word. Keisha took a few steps backward and addressed Nikki. "Would it hurt to put the damn tissue roll on the holder? I told you all the time that I'm not your damn maid."

The dog next door started barking and Nikki looked out the living room window, dismissing Keisha from her vision. A man got out of a cable van, slamming the door, and the dog barked even harder. A minute ago the rain was just pouring but now it had slowed down to a drizzle. The man tried to run for cover when the documents he had in his hand fell to the ground in a puddle of water.

"Damn!" the man swore. He quickly picked up the papers to avoid getting them wet, but it was already too late. "Fuck! Fuck!" He was infuriated. He turned his attention to the barking dog. "Fuck you, too!" His phone started to ring in his pocket and he answered it. "What is it?" he answered angrily. Whatever the person on the other end said to him made him hiss through his teeth. He ran back to the vehicle and retrieved a new set of papers, then slammed the door with such force it made the dog bark again.

"Shut the hell up, you damn stupid mutt!" he yelled, but that only fueled the dog to bark even more. He turned his body, stepping off the sidewalk, but quickly took a step back to avoid getting hit by an oncoming car. The car pulled into the driveway of the barking mutt, which made the dog scratch at the window in excitement. He turned his head to view the luxurious car.

A smile was plastered on Nikki's face, knowing he could never afford a car like that any day soon. Pep. Pep! The man secured his expensive car by pressing his alarm button. He had a smirk on his face, knowing the cable man wouldn't mind taking it for a spin.

"You motherfucker," the cable man said at his audacity.

The man ran to the door, shielding his head with his briefcase. His expensive Armani suit and shoes confirmed his wealth.

"That alarm can't save your damn car if I told my Puerto Rican friend where to find it." The cable man dashed across the street and surprisingly he was heading to Nikki. She turned her attention back to her books, not wanting him to see her looking.

Ding-dong, the doorbell chimed. She figured Keisha would get the door since she was the one who was always expecting packages and visitors; and, besides, Nikki was consumed with her books, studying for her finals to be a cardio surgeon. Ding-dong. Ding-dong. The doorbell chimed relentlessly. Keisha was nowhere in sight. The man banged the door with his fist, assuming the doorbell was broken. "Sometimes I think I'm the damn house-keeper," Nikki hissed thought her teeth as she got up from the couch to open the door.

The man did a combination of pounding and pressing the doorbell, which made Nikki furious. She opened the door as the man was in motion to pound the door and his hand froze in midair. "Can I help you?" Nikki greeted him with an attitude of a wild pit bull. Her nipples poked through her tight-fitted white T-shirt with the words BABY PHAT written across her chest, exposing the fact that she had no bra on.

His facial expression said it all. He wanted to rip her blouse off and greet her nipples with his warm tongue. It was as if her chest were her face because his eyes were intensely focused on her breasts. *If I was your man all the things I'd do to you,* Mark thought as he licked his lips like LL Cool J.

"How may I help you?" Her voice interrupted his fantasy.

He brought his attention to her face and she stared intently at him. "You are more beautiful than I thought."

"What did you just say?"

He cleared his throat and refocused on what he came there to do. "I'm here to fix the cable." He no longer wanted to tend to his job. He had a new job in mind and that was to make her his woman.

"By the way you were pounding the door I would have thought your job would be of some importance."

He smiled, revealing his teeth; they were well maintained, as if he habitually visited the dentist. His smile would have melted your heart. He was very handsome and stereotypically could be tossed in the Mr. Playa, Playa pile.

"May I come inside?"

"Wait right here." She looked him up and down, trying to size him up. She gave him a look of uncertainty before closing the door.

She must think I'm a damn serial killer. Mark brought his attention back to the car across the street. The Porsche sat beautifully in the driveway. He pictured himself driving a car like that one day, but his would be black instead of silver with tinted windows. He imagined himself cruising on I-95 with the woman he just met next to him. Several minutes had passed when he came back to reality and looked at his watch. *I know she couldn't possibly forget that I'm standing out here.*

He raised his arm to knock on the door but before he could the door opened and a different face greeted him. She was even more attractive than the woman before.

"I'm Keisha," she stated and posed seductively against the door. It was as if she wanted him to be captivated by her body, but he didn't indulge himself.

"So can I come inside to do my job now?" He didn't give her the attention she sought because even though she was beautiful something about the first woman was tantalizing.

"Follow me," she said with an attitude as she tightened the string around her pink terry-cloth robe. She led the way and he followed. But he paused for a second, checking out her ass. Her ass cheeks slapped each other as she walked. After all, only a blind man could refuse to look. He knew under that robe she had a body like Beyoncé. She turned to see his eyes fixated on her ass. "Are you coming?"

"Your behind." He cleared his throat. "I mean I'm right behind you."

He followed her to the living room, where the woman he made love to in his fantasy was now sitting with the company of many books; but she didn't even acknowledge his presence.

"The cable box is right here, and I think you already met Nikki," Keisha stated as she exited the room, rolling her eyes at Nikki.

He was captivated by Nikki. Even with the attitude she possessed her true beauty radiated from inside out. He fumbled with a couple of wires but his attention kept shifting to Nikki, causing him to drop his equipment on the floor, disrupting her concentration. Nikki shook her head, obviously annoyed by his presence. "I'm sorry about that." He hastily picked up his tool. Nikki looked at him with disgust.

Her attitude was turning him on. He wanted to walk over and take the book out of her hand, lift her shirt up, and release her breasts. He wanted to greet her erect nipples with his warm tongue and kiss all over her body, not missing a spot. Loud laughter erupted from the TV, frightening him back to reality. "I guess my job here is done."

"Couldn't be fast enough." She raised her head from her book. "You know your way to the door."

He walked over to Nikki, wiping his hand on his pants then stretching it forward with the gesture for a hand-shake. "My name is Mark," he said in a baritone voice, but his gesture was ignored. "So you can't spare a minute to talk to me?"

"If you can't see, let my words be your guide." She spoke slowly as if she were speaking to an adolescent. "I am studying in order to get a good job, so I don't have to be bothered with men like you, who obviously think that every woman is in a desperate need for a man."

Her reply wasn't what he expected. Her words shattered his ego. Mark stepped back without responding. He gathered his tools and proceeded to the door, but suddenly stopped and turned to face her. "Women like you never give a good man a chance, then you cry to your friends that there are no good men left out there. Yes, I'm a cable guy, but I have dreams and goals just like you."

Nikki didn't hesitate to respond. It was as if she was giving him a beating with her tongue. "What are your dreams? To buy a Benz, with nowhere to park it! What are your goals? Let me guess: to have every woman wanting to drive in the front seat of your car."

"So because I'm not in a business suit you are stereo-typing me. Why can't I be a man who wants to better for my life just like you? That's the problem with women like you."

She was obviously offended by his comment. She walked over to him and spoke with authority. "Women like me! Do you know my struggle? Do you know how hard it is to find a decent job without a college degree? So, yes, a woman like me decides to go back to school to better myself, so excuse me if I have no time to socialize with people like you." She pointed her index finger at him. "You know your way out." She looked at him like he was scum on the ground.

Mark was insulted but he liked the fact that she was confident, focused, and took no bullshit from no one. He didn't mind that she was chewing him up and spitting him out. Usually Mark would break a woman down like an old bench with a fat man sitting on it, but he was no match for this fiery pit bull and he liked it.

"With all due respect, I think you're a nice woman if you get rid of your attitude; but to be honest I like your confidence. Can I take you out sometime?"

"Ha, ha!" Nikki laughed out loud as if she were at a comedy show and heard the funniest joke. "Your confidence doesn't suit you. Do you honestly think that I would go on a date with you? A woman like me needs a man to commend me for doing better, not talk down to me for wanting better." She looked over her shoulder at him as she exited the room, leaving him startled at her wittiness.

"Is everything okay?" Keisha came strolling back to the room.

Mark ignored Keisha's question and leaned his head to get a better view of Nikki as she walked away. She was out of his sight; then he brought his attention to Keisha. "Did you say something?"

"So how much do I owe you?" She got closer to him, looking directly into his eyes as if she were trying to hypnotize him.

He turned and walked toward the door. "This one is on me, if you can get your friend to go on a date with me."

Keisha followed him to the door. Mark stepped outside but then turned and gave Keisha his card. "Have your friend call me when she decides to take a break from studying." Mark descended the steps, running to his van.

Keisha hastily walked to the kitchen, where Nikki was pouring milk into a bowl of Frosted Flakes cereal. "So what do you think about Mark?" Keisha asked.

"What is there to think about? He's not my type."

Keisha shook her head. "What exactly is your type?"

Nikki had a big smile on her face. "All is need is my books."

"You are as dull and dreary as the weather outside."

The sun, all of a sudden, emerged from behind the clouds and brightened the kitchen. "I beg to differ."

Keisha rolled her eyes and walked out the kitchen to her bedroom.

Chapter 2

The gold-plated metals that accentuated Keisha's king-sized canopy bed sparkled. "I have to change these damn curtains," she stated as she made her way over to the window, trying to prevent the excess light from seeping through the sheer gold embroidered curtains. The light reflected off her Chanel, Juicy Couture, and many other name-brand perfume bottles, and it danced on her bed, mocking her attempt to block out the sun; and her efforts were in vain.

"I can already tell that today is going to be a bad day for me." She shook her head, accepting defeat. Suddenly having a craving for some orange juice, she shook her head and headed back to the kitchen. She took the carton of SunnyD from the fridge and poured herself a glass, but got distracted by the blinking light on her answering machine that indicated she had awaiting messages. She continued pouring while she stretched her free hand to press the play button. Her glass overflowed and she felt the cold juice on her feet.

"Damn it!" She stomped her feet. She removed her feet from her wet, furry slippers. Hopping on one leg she retrieved a paper towel and wiped her foot.

"You have two new messages," the machine stated when she pressed the retrieve button. The first message was for Nikki and she erased it after the first few words.

"Keisha, don't forget to meet me . . ." It was her friend Shay reminding her that they had business to take care of. She walked off with the glass of orange juice while the message still played. She put the glass to her lips and didn't remove it until the glass was empty, setting it on the granite sink in the bathroom afterwards. The green and gold decoration gave the bathroom a warm feel. Keisha took pride in keeping her bathroom squeaky clean because that was her zone to relax and unwind. Taking a bubble bath with a magazine, looking at the latest fashion, was something that was done as her therapy.

The water temperature was gauged to warm before she undressed herself, revealing her naked body. She placed a pink shower cap on her head, then stepped in the tub. Today she didn't have time for a bubble bath because she was running behind time to meet up with Shay. "Just what I needed," she said approvingly as the warm water escaped the shower head and greeted her body. A flashback on the date she had a few days ago almost dampened her spirit. *That sick bastard.* The water glided down her body, relaxing her muscles, and she exhaled, wishing she could rid herself of the memory of that horrible date.

It was around eight o'clock when Keisha got to the restaurant and walked over to David's table, where he was already seated, drinking his tequila. David wore an Armani suit, and Keisha thought it had better be expensive because she could tell the real from the fake at a quick glance. She stood for a second to see if he would show her the courtesy of getting up and pulling out her chair, but he didn't. Raising his glass was his way of greeting her. He had an attitude, as if Keisha being late was his biggest pet peeve. Keisha stood with her hand on her hip, irritated by his mannerisms.

"I ordered for you since I was hungry and you were an hour late," he said as he put the glass to his head.

"Since you're so hungry, why don't you have both meals? I'm sure that I wouldn't enjoy what you ordered anyways."

She turned to walk away but he stood up and grabbed her arm, letting her know that he still needed her company. She looked down at her wrist, then looked back at him, indicating that he needed to release her hand. He quickly obliged, raising both his hands for a truce. Keisha stepped away from the table, turned off by his attitude.

"Wait a minute."

She stopped and turned to face him.

"I like that you have some fire in you. Let's start over. Since this is a five-star restaurant you can order anything you want on the menu. It's my treat."

"Is that supposed to make me smile from ear-to-ear as if I'm not acquainted with fine dining?"

David made a few huge sales in real estate and now he thought he was Donald Trump or God's gift to women. In fact he was a small fry in comparison to some of the men she was dating. Yes, you heard right, some of the men. Keisha took a deep breath and exhaled aloud. As she walked back to the table her blood was boiling. She couldn't stand a man who was on his high horse thinking he was God's gift to woman.

Their table was close to the kitchen and she could hear the ruckus that was going on back there. It was like an episode of Hell's Kitchen. *She pulled out the chair and sat down and her eyes begin to wander from table to table. Keisha frequently dined at this restaurant but never was it full to capacity like tonight. As she continued scanning the room, tuning out whatever David was yapping about, her eyes locked on to the Jamaican Olympic track star Usain Bolt dining with a few reggae artists.*

The ringing of David's phone caused her to bring her attention to him. "Hello," he answered with a smile. He was instructing someone to meet him at the restaurant and Keisha was about to spit fire. "See you in a few." David ended his conversation.

"What was that about?"

"I'm having an old friend of mine dining with us, that's all."

This motherfucker must be crazy. How the hell is he going to invite someone on our date? On second thought his friend is probably more my type anyway. I could just slip him my number and see what he has to offer.

Keisha was enjoying her steak more than she was enjoying David's company. He was blabbing about his new Ferrari.

"Is your friend in real estate too?" Keisha cut him off in midsentence.

"No," he replied and tried to carry on his conversation, praising his car. She didn't want to hear about how expensive the car was, nor was she fascinated by his description of the posh leather interior. He was admiring his car more than he was admiring her and she was right there in his presence. Who wouldn't want to compliment me or beg for my attention? *David was in love with his new car and she was jealous.*

"So, is he a childhood friend?" Keisha inquired, but her attention shifted while he replied to her question. She was incoherent of his words because of the woman walking toward their table, strutting her stuff in a dress by Dolce & Gabbana: the same dress she planed on ordering when she saw it in a magazine. There was no denying that the woman was stunning. The knee-length pink spaghetti-strap dress hugged the woman's figure. Her ample bosom, which looked to be a thirty-eight C, sat perfectly on her chest. They were surely bought and paid for. Keisha brought her attention back to her plate, not wanting to stare at the woman any longer because the green-eyed monster would start to show. Not many women could size up to Keisha but tonight she saw her competition.

"What were you saying about your friend?" she said, raising her glass to her lips, which were heavily moistened with lip gloss. *The outline of her lips remained on the rim with a slight tinge of pink when she set the glass back on the table.*

"She is right here."

"She?" Keisha asked with a quick turn of her head. She was under the assumption that David's friend would be a male.

David got up from his seat and greeted the woman with a tight embrace. Keisha quickly took another sip of her wine to wash the filet mignon down so she wouldn't choke.

"Keisha, this is my old friend Lisa I was telling you about." David introduced the woman with pride. She was the same woman wearing the designer dress that Keisha was just admiring.

Oh hell no. *The date was already going sour but now the presence of this woman joining them put a bitter taste in her mouth. Keisha had lost her appetite. She wanted to toss her drink in his face and couldn't have cared less if she ruined the bitch's expensive dress. The woman was all over David as if he was a long-lost lover or she was a bitch for hire who he paid well.*

The waiter brought an extra chair and David fixed it at the table, then made sure that Lisa was properly seated. Look at this shit. He didn't even pull my damn chair. Now I definitely have to get to the bottom of this shit.

"Are you two lovers or just friends?" she blurted without delay.

"I would say just friends," the woman replied while gazing into David's eyes. She wiped his cheek, removing her lip gloss that was placed there from her kiss.

"Is that more like friends with benefit?" Keisha suspiciously asked.

"David, I think someone is getting jealous," Lisa sang in an annoying voice.

Bitch, please, I might be pissed about the fact that you are wearing the dress I wanted but certainly not jealous of you and him. All I want is to get close to his pocket, not him.

The waiter returned to refill their glasses but Keisha opted for something stronger because she wanted to calm her nerves. She wanted to explode on them but she held her composure and remained classy.

"Cîroc pineapple," Keisha ordered with a smile on her face.

David took the extra plate that wasn't touched and placed it in front of Lisa. "Oh, salmon is my favorite." Without hesitation, she picked up the fork and indulged.

I guess he ordered it for your ass because I definitely don't like salmon.

"So, did David tell you about his new Ferrari?" she asked while still chewing.

"Yes, but a Bentley is more on my level."

"Where did you find this one? She has expensive taste."

"Where did he find me?" Keisha raised her voice, turning a few heads.

"Calm down." David tried to defuse her. "She didn't mean anything by it."

The waiter returned with Keisha's order of Cîroc pineapple. It couldn't have been better timing. She took a big gulp, almost finishing her drink in one shot.

David sat with his arms folded on his chest, intently viewing both women. He was feeling like a king. He was getting satisfaction from having two beautiful women wanting him.

Lisa and David caught up on old times as if Keisha weren't even at the table. The woman gave him goggle *eyes as she laughed at his jokes that weren't even funny. Why the hell am I still here? It's obvious that three is a crowd. Keisha wiped her mouth with the white napkin, staining it with her pink lip gloss. She reached for her Louis V. purse in her lap, finding her lip gloss to reapply. A little freshening up before she made her exit.*

"So, ladies, what's for dessert?" *David rubbed his hands together.*

"I don't think she will go for it," *Lisa added as they both stared at Keisha.*

"Let me handle it," *David said with confidence. He went into his pocket and took out a stack of money and placed it in front of Keisha.*

She looked at him questioningly with her brow frowned. "What the hell is that for?"

David got up from his chair and walked behind Keisha, resting his hands on both of her shoulders, massaging them gently. "That's my way of apologize for my attitude earlier and hoping that after dinner you will join us at the hotel for dessert. So what will it be?"

Keisha stood up from her chair, enraged. "Do I look like a fucking whore? Take your money and shove it up her ass. How about eating that for dessert?" *Keisha took the remainder of her drink and tossed it into Lisa's lap.*

"You bitch!" *Lisa yelled, causing people to stare.*

"No, honey, that's you." *Keisha walked out of the restaurant like a model on a runway, holding her head high, refraining from bringing out the ghetto in her. She didn't want to be stereotyped as the ghetto black girl in a fancy restaurant. Besides, a few high rollers had their eyes on her. And she wanted to remain a lady.*

The continuous ringing of the doorbell played an awful tune. She tried to ignore it but the person wouldn't go away, which resulted in her ending her shower. She grabbed her robe and covered herself, then hastily walked to the door like a madwoman. There was a woman she didn't recognize standing at her door.

"May I help you?"

"Where is he? I know he's in there!" the angry woman yelled as she tried to see past her by tipping up on her toes, swaying from side to side.

If it was any other morning Keisha would have enjoyed putting her in her place, but not this morning. She didn't know this woman and she didn't care to know who she was or what she was being accused of. After viewing her from head to toe, Keisha shook her head and slammed the door in her face. It wasn't unusual for a wife to come knocking at her door whenever her husband didn't come home at night. Keisha would always feel the wrath of the sanctimonious bitches whether or not she was guilty of the crime.

"Charles, I know you are in there!" the woman shouted as she banged on the door. The boisterous woman had her neighbors' curiosity running wild. You could see them peeping out their windows to see what was going on.

This was a quiet and quaint neighborhood located in Bridgeport, Connecticut, an hour away from New York. The neighbors' lawns were always well manicured, with luxurious cars in each driveway showing off their wealth; but that was also a cover-up to hide their miserable and unhappy lives. You would see wives running errands with their fancy designer handbags occasionally waving to their neighbors and giving a phony smile. They all feared Keisha because their husbands secretly lusted after her and she had a reputation for crossing boundaries to get whatever she wanted. Keisha didn't care much for the people who lived in the neighborhood but she wasn't going to give them the satisfaction of seeing her leave.

Keisha moved to the neighborhood when Martin up-rooted her from the Bronx. Her apartment, off White

Plains Road at 228th and Carpenter, was her paradise until she met Martin one day when she went shopping in the city.

She accidentally walked into Martin because she was gazing at a Chanel pocketbook that she couldn't afford. "I'm so sorry." She tried to get by him on the busy sidewalk.

"All is forgiven if you let me purchase that pocketbook for you."

Keisha slowed her steps and looked over her shoulder to view him. She was tempted by his offer. But she decided to keep walking.

He caught up with her and kept up with her pace. "I mean no harm. I just hate to see a beautiful woman not getting what she wants."

Keisha noticed his expensive suit and immediately knew she wanted to spend some of his money.

"How about if we go to lunch in a public place so you can get to know me better?"

Keisha thought about the Chanel pocketbook and how badly she wanted it, but decided to play it safe. "No, thank you."

Martin nodded his head in approval. He reached in his pocket and pulled out his business card. "Well, here is my card. You can call me anytime."

Keisha took his card and walked away, disappearing in the Manhattan rush-hour crowd.

Two months after dialing Mr. Martin Graham's number, Keisha was living in Connecticut with her sugar daddy. He wanted her closer to him even though he was married and lived a few blocks down with his wife and kids. But since he was paying the bills she went along for the ride. People would whisper about their affair but she couldn't care less. But this morning after his wife stormed into her bedroom she knew whatever was left of her reputation would be tarnished. All the neighborhood wives would now put their husbands on a tight leash knowing Keisha was a home wrecker. Martin's wife would take Martin for all he had, leaving him with nothing; but Keisha was no fool. She had blackmailed Martin into paying off her condo, or else she would go public with the videos she made of him and his crazy fantasies. Besides, the condo was already in her name. She knew what she wanted and how to get it.

Now it would be a ritual for insecure wives to come knocking at her door, looking for their husbands. Like this crazy bitch who was still banging her door. Keisha was going to have a field day telling them how great their husbands were in bed for her cruel satisfaction, especially if she was being accused of an affair that she had nothing to do with. She was going to enjoy knocking them off their high pedestals, but this morning she didn't have the energy or the time to deal with this bitch.

Keisha poured a bottle of water that was sitting on the counter into the kettle and turned the stove on without acknowledging the verbal attack of a gold digger gone mad outside. These wives weren't in love with their husbands, but in love with the money, so they felt threatened whenever another woman was in the picture. The ringing of her cell phone made her rush to the bedroom. It was sitting on the nightstand playing a song by Drake. "Hey you," she said seductively.

Her persona suddenly changed from monotonous to sensual bliss, followed by a smile from ear to ear. She massaged her leg with a Victoria's Secret lotion and smiled at the words that tainted her mind. Keisha released a big laugh, dismissing the negative energy that had made her morning miserable. "I'll see you then." She ended her conversation.

Standing in front of her walk-in closet trying to decide the outfit for the day wasn't a hard task because she had everything to her comfort. She picked out a white fitted Bebe dress pant with the price tag of $110 still on it. She put her feet in then wiggled it up her legs. The tight-fitted black tank top made her breasts seem as if she had implants. The white fitted blazer made the look complete. She viewed herself in the mirror and saw perfection. Keisha blew herself a kiss. *I feel bad for the people who aren't as beautiful as me.*

She heavily applied her Mac makeup then completed the look with her black Michael K. pumps and matching purse. She took a second glance in the mirror and her beauty was undeniable. "Damn I look good."

She exited the bedroom and sashayed her way to the door. Outside in the driveway her silver BMW awaited her. Keisha covered her eyes with her Gucci shades and turned the keys in the ignition. "She's Royal" by Tarrus Riley started to play. Her cell phone started to ring and it was Tina calling. "Hello," she answered as she backed out of the driveway with one hand on the steering wheel, looking behind her. "I'm on my way."

Chapter 3

Within minutes Keisha was outside Tina's apartment. She blew the car horn. "I knew she wouldn't be ready." She tapped on her horn again. Keisha viewed herself in the mirror to make sure her makeup wasn't flawed. Tina opened the passenger side door and sat in the car. "What took you so long?"

"I had to look as good as you," Tina replied.

Keisha gave her a once-over. "Not even close." She drove off. "Let's go over the plan once again because you seem to lose your head sometimes. If he's not falling for the trap you need to come over and act as if I am a business acquaintance of yours."

"Yes, from *Hustler* magazine!" Tina laughed.

"It's not funny. I know you get nervous around these big shots but you better don't miss my signal."

Keisha and Tina were up to their old tricks as usual. Seeking out prey was their daily ritual. According to them their bodies would make them rich because they already had degrees in hustling suckers for their money. One of their many tactics would be to Google wealthy business-men, then seek out their places of business. Keisha would accidentally bump into him on his way out to lunch. This was a craft that she had perfected.

They entered the lobby of People's Bank headquarters in downtown Bridgeport, wearing their confidence proudly.

"Hello. May I help you?" the receptionist greeted them. They strolled past her to the elevator.

"Ladies, ladies, you have to sign in!"

They proceeded without acknowledging the receptionist. The numbers were counting down on the elevator and Keisha rushed over to the door, awaiting a victim. *Five, four, three, two, one.* She counted down the numbers in her head. Ding! The elevator stopped, and a man exited the elevator, and she stepped into him, dropping the folder she had in her hand, and paper scattered on the floor.

"I'm so sorry," the man said as he gathered up the documents from the ground. He looked up at her.

"Uncle Patrick!" Keisha quickly stepped back. It had been many years since the last time she saw her uncle, and to be reunited in an awkward situation like this. He wasn't supposed to be the one coming out of the elevator. They were both surprised.

"What are you doing here?" Keisha inquired.

"I should be asking you that question." He quickly stood to his feet, speaking in a deep voice that would be fit for a radio personality.

"I'm here for a job interview on the third floor."

"What position? I can put in a good word for you."

"In the fraud department, but I have this job in the bag. My connection, Simone, is going to work her magic."

"Do you mean Mrs. Simone Preston?"

"No, Simone Merkerson." *I can't believe that there is a Simone working here. Well, let's see if there is one with this last name. I really hope he doesn't go inquiring.*

In actuality she never had a job interview. This particular day Keisha's victim was supposed to be the bank executive Mr. Cooper. And Tina was there as a decoy, a companion just in case their plan fell through so it wouldn't seem suspicious. Mr. Cooper was going to be their next meal ticket.

"You have grown into a lovely young lady. I almost didn't recognize you. So now you think that you are too grown to give your uncle a hug."

Keisha gave him a tight squeeze. She missed her uncle dearly. He always came to her defense whenever her father would always chastise her as a child. But to sway the attention from herself, Keisha raked her fingers through her hair, giving Tina the SOS signal. Tina sashayed her way over and Patrick turned his attention to her greeting her with a big smile.

"Tina, this is my Uncle Patrick, the CEO of Top Dot Records."

Tina eyes radiated when she heard the title he held. He stretched his hand forward to greet her with a handshake but Tina embraced him with a tight hug instead.

The elevator door opened and Keisha's attention drifted and she zoomed in on Mr. Cooper. *Make contact, followed by an apology; then get him weak in the knees with seduction.* Keisha went over the steps in her head on how to catch her victim, but today she watched him leave the building, escaping her trap. *Tomorrow is another day. I will get you under my spell.* She brought her attention back to her uncle, and Tina was getting really friendly.

Keisha grabbed her arm, pulling her away, because she wasn't going to let Tina get her claws into her uncle's pocket. Not only that, but Patrick would give Tina whatever she desired and Keisha wasn't going to let that happen. Keisha had to be on top even if that meant holding her friend back. She had no loyalty to anyone. She used people for whatever they could offer her at the moment with no regard for their feelings. She had no female friends except for Tina, who was her rookie in training. Keisha didn't mind her tagging along or sharing the spotlight because Keisha called the shots. Tina only got whatever or whoever Keisha didn't want. Tina idolized Keisha and wouldn't want to feel her wrath if she was to go against her.

"Tina was just leaving to go meet up with a client for lunch," Keisha informed Patrick.

"I was?" Tina asked in confusion.

Keisha grabbed her arm, leading her to the door. "My uncle is off-limits." She hastily rejoined her uncle with her arms open wide and embraced him with a hug. "I'm so happy to see you, Uncle."

Keisha wasn't family oriented. She had no family values. The only things valuable to her were her clothes and jewelry. She hadn't seen her family in years, ever since she ran away from home as a teenager. Keisha was from a middle-class family. Her father was a lawyer and her mother was a social worker. Her father was a stern man who ruled with an iron fist. There was nothing more important than getting an education and he wanted his daughter to follow in his footsteps. But Keisha had different plans for her life, none that her father would ever approve of. She wanted to get away from her father's rules and laws, but in order for her to do that she needed money and she knew exactly where to get it. On her seventeenth birthday she conjured up a plan to blackmail her father's business partner into giving her a large sum of money. It wasn't hard for her to pull it off and it took little planning. He was a married man with a lust for younger girls and she used it to her advantage. She convinced him to meet with her and it would be their little secret. He fell for it and honestly it didn't take much convincing. Once she had him where she wanted him, she took incriminating pictures of him. She threatened to send them to his wife and showed them to her father if he didn't comply with her wishes. She wanted $35,000 for her silence and he gave it to her with no hesitation. That was just the beginning of her many schemes to come.

There were two empty chairs in the fancy decorated lobby. Keisha led her uncle to sit. He was in awe to see her all grown up. She was now thirty years old and no longer his little niece. She was now a grown woman. They chitchatted about their lives and she even elaborated on her pretend job as an editor at the nonexistent magazine company she was working for. She didn't want him to know that she was a schemer because he would be so disappointed in her. Keisha knew her uncle was a cash machine and she wasn't going to let him leave without getting him to write her a fat check.

At this point she regretted cutting her uncle out her life. But she felt as if to get a clean break from her father she had to cut all ties with everyone. She didn't want anyone giving up her whereabouts. But now she was a grown woman who was no longer in hiding.

"Uncle, I'm tapped out of money and I need help with my rent."

Patrick didn't hesitate; he quickly took out his check-book. "Fill in the amount you need." She did as she was told with a smile on her face. She passed the checkbook back to him and he chuckled. "That's a lot of money!"

"That's just loose change to you."

Patrick adjusted his tie and cleared his throat. He filled out the check then ripped it out of the checkbook. Keisha stretched her hand forward but Patrick put the check into his pocket. Keisha wore a look of confusion.

"I have a business proposition and I think you have the perfect skill for the job."

"Job?" she repeated as if she didn't hear him clearly. The word gave her an instant migraine. Keisha never had a job, nor was she interested in having one. She always depended on her looks and so far she was doing great. Keisha had men eating out of the palm of her hand and for her selfish pleasure. She viewed her manicure nails and the thought of doing work made her want to hurl. "But I already have a job."

Patrick patted her hand. "This is a weekend position and you already have the skills for the job."

Keisha wrinkled her brow in curiosity. "A magazine editor?" She searched his face for an answer.

"No. Something more exciting."

Keisha pouted her lips and squeezed them together. "You got my attention."

He held her hand in his. "There are a few young talents that I want to sign to my label but there are two who are playing hardball."

"I don't see where I fit in."

"Simple, your job will be to get him to sign with my label."

"I'm listening." She adjusted her body to face him.

"All you have to do is go to a party or two and get their attention and convince them to sign."

"How would I do that? I know nothing about the business."

"You are underestimating yourself. You are very attractive and that's good enough."

"I'm still not following." Keisha shook her head from side to side and pushed her shoulders upward.

"Okay, listen. These entertainers have a weakness for beautiful women. Look at you. How would they be able to resist?"

"Now you are speaking my language. This is a position that I'm more than willing to accept, so when do I start?" Her eyes were glowing and excitement took over her body.

"I know I would be able to count on you but under no circumstance can they know that you are my niece."

"I have no problem with that. I can reel them in on my own."

"Well if you can reel Bling in I'll owe you big. He has a little island flava. The other artist I also need to sign, his name is Hype. He's young but he has what it takes to sell albums."

"How young are we talking? I look too good to go to jail, especially for seducing a minor."

"Come on, Keisha, you are my niece. I wouldn't put you in a predicament like that."

"How young is he?"

"Twenty-three," he said while coughing.

"Seriously, Uncle, no, I won't. Seem as if you forgot that I'm thirty years old."

"Come on, he is way over twenty-one. Beside he's a hothead and loves a pretty woman. I see him in action at the clubs."

"So why don't you just throw in a few more dollars on the signing bonus and maybe you can catch him that way?"

"I've tried but he's not biting. Everybody is talking about doing independent records. It's taking money from my pocket. Do you know what a hit song does for my pocket?

I can only imagine what you are going to do for my pocket. If I bring these artists to him he will bring the Benjamins to me. After all, "it's all about the Benjamins, baby."

"Once they sign on the dotted line, then and only then you can have that five thousand dollar check."

"C.O.D. Cash on delivery."

"You have the mentality of a hustler. I like that. So are you going to give me your friend's number?"

Keisha got up and hung her pocketbook over her shoulder. "She's a gold digger."

"I have some loose change to spare." They both laughed.

Keisha departed from her uncle, exuding confidence because she was up for the challenge. Keisha walked to the parking lot where Tina was awaiting her in the car. But before she could get her foot in the car Tina lashed out at her. "Why the hell did you dismiss me like that?" Tina questioned.

"I wanted to talk to my uncle in private. Is there a problem?" Keisha searched her for answers. "Are you interested in my uncle?" Keisha laughed and refreshed her lip gloss in the mirror.

"What if I am?"

"Don't waste your time because you are not on his level."

"What the fuck is that supposed to mean?" Tina was disturbed by Keisha's statement. "Are you saying I'm not good enough to date your uncle?"

Tina's persona changed as she stared at Keisha with a look of dismay, but Keisha looked at her and laughed even harder. "Are you serious? Do you honestly think that you are on his level?"

"And what level is that?"

Keisha flipped the mirror up. "You know you're not wife material."

Tina was infuriated and hurt by the statement. She put her shades on because her eyes told exactly what her heart felt at the moment. Keisha drove out of the parking lot and turned her music up. Tina sat in her seat as an obedient child. Yes, her feelings were hurt, but she knew better than to prolong the conversation. It was as if she was in a cult and Keisha was the leader or she was under a spell. She idolized Keisha and Keisha's word was the law. Tina dismissed her anger and replaced it with the tainted belief that Keisha was right.

They left the bank and headed to Rootsman Kitchen to get some Jamaican food; but Keisha suddenly changed her mind and quickly jammed on her brakes to do a three-point turn.

"Are you trying to kill me?" Tina screamed as she placed her hand on the dashboard to brace herself from going through the windshield because she wasn't wearing her seat belt.

"I just remembered I have to run to the mall." Keisha had taken the offer from her uncle and she had to find the perfect dress that would have this guy drooling like a puppy. She had no doubt in herself that she would have him in her uncle's office ready to sign on the dotted line. She was now driving up Park Avenue approaching the light at Park and Capital. She made the right turn even though the sign clearly stated NO TURN ON RED. She crossed over Madison and was now at Capital and Main, sitting at the light.

She looked over at Tina to see if she had falling asleep because she wasn't saying a word. Her eyes were wide open but Keisha could tell that Tina would have rather been somewhere else than hanging with her at this moment, but Keisha knew Tina didn't have the guts to speak her mind.

Keisha viewed her makeup in the rearview mirror for the second time. The light had turned green and the car behind her honked for her to go. She stuck her middle finger up and accelerated at her convenience.

A big sign that highlighted Westfield Shopping Mall Trumbull stood high for all to see. Keisha got into her left lane turning into the mall entrance. The parking lot was crowded for the simple reason that it was Friday afternoon and everyone was trying to find an outfit for the weekend. She drove into a few rows before seeing a car pulling out of a space. She noticed another car waiting for the spot but that wasn't going to stop her from getting it. Keisha swung into the space before the car that was already waiting could get it.

"You fucking bitch!" the lady hollered.

Keisha laughed and put her car in park. The lady was heated. She called Keisha every name possible. Keisha got out of the car and the woman was in a rage.

"I should run over your stupid ass," she hollered out the window.

"Take your sloppy ass home," Tina said in Keisha's defense.

Keisha entered the mall with her head held high and treated the hallway as a runway. The shoppers and window shoppers were her audience. Keisha summoned Tina to be her personal assistant. Express was her first stop.

"I need that one, that one, and this one." Tina found Keisha sizes in the dresses she pointed to. She didn't attempt to enter the fitting room because she didn't have to second-guess her size. She was confident that every item would be a perfect fit. Tina was step-by-step with Keisha to the register and placed the dresses on the counter.

"I'll take all these."

The cashier had a suspicious look on her face. "Are you aware that these are our newest arrivals and they are not on sale?"

"But I know that you are. What street corner do you work on after work?" she snapped back at the cashier.

The cashier irately scanned the items and tossed them into the shopping bags. She announced the total to be $448. "Will that be credit?" she asked with an attitude, rolling her eyes.

"No, bitch, cash." Keisha took $500 out of her purse and placed it on the counter. "Keep the change, bitch!" She took her bags and walked away.

Keisha paid for everything with cash. She also liked to see the looks on everyone's faces when she racked up a big bill and paid for everything with cash. It gave her a natural high to see their mouths open wide and their eyes turn green with envy. It was a known fact that most women hated her but secretly wanted to be like her. She leisurely walked into every store and exited with multiple bags.

Victoria's Secret was the last stop on her list. She liked to show off her body not only in public but also in the bedroom. She purchased several fragrances and lingerie of all colors and styles before leaving the store. Her phone started to ring in her pocketbook and she struggled to get it. She had more shopping bags than she had hands to carry them. A man stood talking on his phone in the hallway and she summoned him to assist her.

"Why don't you make yourself useful and hold my bags?"

He quickly ended his phone call and ran to her rescue as if he was under her spell. She got to her cell phone and answered it.

"Hi, Uncle. Don't worry, the plan is still in motion." She bolted into another store and Tina and the man walked behind her like dogs following their master.

"Actually, I just bought the perfect outfit. He definitely won't be able to resist this time." She pointed to a necklace and the man picked it up for her. They walked to the register. "He will sign on the dotted lines. I can promise you that."

"That will be $99.99. Will that be cash or credit?" the cashier said.

Keisha turned to the man. "Will that be cash or credit?"

The man stuttered his words and replied, "Cred . . . credit." He took out his wallet and swiped his card.

Keisha walked out of the store, still talking on her phone. "You can count on me. You owe me big time plus a tip."

She finished her conversation and the man followed them to the car. She wrote on a piece of paper, folded it, and gave it to the man, then drove off. He wore a big smile as he unfolded the paper. His smile quickly faded as he read the note:

You should be grateful that I let you carry my bags.

Keisha's iPhone rang in her pocketbook and she told Tina to get it. Tina shuffled through makeup and other personal items before she found the phone. "It's Nikki," Tina said.

"Ask her what the hell her boring ass wants."

"Hi, Nikki. What's up, girl?" She paused to hear what Nikki had to say. "Nikki wants to know if you need anything from the diner."

"The diner. Even her meals are boring. No, thank you, Mother Teresa."

Chapter 4

Nikki ended the conversation with Tina and held her hand up, signaling a waiter. She was ready to place her order. Hunger had consumed her. She was at the library studying since the sun came up and hadn't eaten yet. The diner wasn't full to capacity. You could count on one hand the amount of people who sat down for lunch. A young couple shared a kiss and a middle-aged man sat by himself, eating a sandwich. Her eyes met with his and he blew a kiss at her. She quickly turned her head and was greeted by the waiter.

"Will you be having your regular?"

She nodded in agreement. Nikki frequented the diner and her order was the same every time: a chicken salad with fries and a Sprite. Yes, you could call her plain Jane, the procrastinator, and you could toss in goody-goody. A man entered the diner, talking on his phone with his conversation on high. She looked up only to see that it was Mark. She hid her face with a book, hoping that he didn't see her, because she had no intention of ever holding a conversation with him again.

Mark and his friend Allan walked past her table, but Mark recognized the book and made a U-turn when he realized that it was Nikki. "We meet again. Is it fate or coincidence?"

She dropped her arm, revealing her face. "Neither, but once again, I'm rudely interrupted. How may I help you?"

Mark was intrigued by her. This was his second chance to make a good impression. He wanted to take her attention from her books that now had turned into the only things that mattered to her.

"I passed by your street a couple of time hoping to catch a glimpse of you but you never grace me with your beauty."

She rolled her eyes, uninterested in his shallow conversation. "Do I need to call the police to report a stalker?"

He smiled. "I'm here to have lunch just like you; or maybe you're thinking I'm here to try to get you to go out on a date with me."

"Isn't that the reason why you are interrupting me?"

"So you can tell me again how much I don't stand a chance with you?"

"Maybe you are hoping that my no will turn into a yes." Mark sat down at the table and held on to her hand and she pulled away her arm. "I'm positive that I didn't give you an invite to join me for lunch."

"Can you explain to me why an attractive woman like you is sitting here dining by yourself? You don't have to say it but I know you need my company."

"That is very presumptuous of you; I am expecting someone to meet me at any minute so I would advise you to leave before he gets here."

A man entered the diner and Nikki waved her hand to get his attention. Mark turned and looked at the man, trying to size up the man in her life. He wasn't much of a character. He didn't picture him to be her type. You would get the impression that he didn't care about his appearance.

"No way that's your man," Mark said disapprovingly.

She waved to him again. This time she had a big smile on her face. Mark got up to leave but he saw the man's female companion greet him with a kiss. Mark turned his head quickly to face Nikki but she didn't make eye contact. The waiter came with her meal and she took up her fork and started eating her salad. The man walked past her table with his companion and she gulped her soda and choked. She felt embarrassed and humiliated. She wanted to be submerged in her seat. She wished she could disappear.

"Was that . . ." Mark pointed in the man's direction.

"Wrong person."

"So you don't know what your man looks like? Or maybe that was really him with another woman."

She didn't have a witty comeback this time but she knew she couldn't let him get to her. "I don't have to answer to you."

"But he will answer to me." Mark got up from around the table.

She couldn't let him go over there to that man's table to defend her or otherwise. She had to stop him. "What are you doing? You can't go over there." She held on to his shirt. She had to do something. She couldn't let him humiliate her because, after all, she didn't know the man. It was a hoax to get him to leave and now it backfired on her.

"Okay, okay. I'm not expecting any company. I lied."

Mark turned around with a smile on his face. "I knew it! You are a bad liar. Do you honestly think I would go make a fool of myself?"

"You are a selfish, self-centered jerk!"

Mark laughed.

Nikki had now lost her appetite. She pushed the meal aside. The joke was on her. "I don't appreciate you having a laugh at my expense. You are immature and shallow."

"You are the one who started this and it backfired on you and now you are attacking me. Lighten up. Where is your sense of humor?"

The tables had turned and she was the butt of the joke. Deep inside she wanted to laugh but she wouldn't dare let him see a smile on her face. She wanted to remain a tough cookie. She wasn't going to let him in that easy; besides, sharing a joke with him would mean she had let down her guard. He would have to earn it.

"Did you see the size of that guy? He would have knocked me out without even trying."

"Are you ready to order, sir?" the waiter revisited the table to take Mark order.

"I'll have the grilled chicken breast sandwich to go and make the bread toasted."

Mark was sporting an expensive watch. Something a cable guy would think twice about purchasing if he had bills to pay or a family to support. Nikki didn't think much of it only because she had dubbed him to be a shallow, materialistic man, so that was expected of him. Mark was a very handsome man. His smile would have made a cold-hearted person become compassionate. He had a fresh haircut that enhanced his facial structure. He was close to six feet in height and you could tell he had a perfect body under his tunic. Nikki's mind started to wander because his cologne was masculine but wasn't overbearing to the nostrils. It was sending signals to her body parts that were now gravitating towards his.

She sipped on her soda, dismissing the urges. "Are you hoping to score points by pretending to be a gentleman? I can see though this false pretense. You are so predict-able."

"There is a lot about me that you don't know. Don't be too quick to judge a book by its cover, Miss College Student." He picked up her book, turning through the pages.

"Are you saying that there is more to you than your dull appearance?"

"Is there more to you than your shallow way of thinking?"

"You said you had goals and dreams. I wouldn't mind hearing how superficial they are."

"Sorry to disappoint you but look at the time. I have to get back to my menial job as a cable guy. Give me a call. Maybe I can take you out on a real date and we could talk about my superficial goals then." Mark exited the restaurant, knowing he got her right where he wanted her.

Nikki watched him walks away. She was intrigued by him but wouldn't dare admit it to herself or especially to him. In the past other guys would walk away without a fight because they lacked the confidence to go up against an intelligent woman. Mark was witty and she liked the challenge.

Nikki didn't have a man because she didn't have the patience to deal with their adolescent mentality or their ignorance; besides, she got her heart broken so many times before. She had given up on finding her Mr. Right but something about Mark intrigued her.

Outside was a scorching eighty degrees. She wanted to call Keisha for a ride but decided against it. The thought of getting home to some peace and quiet made her welcome the idea of taking public transportation. Her 2001 Ford Escape was in the shop, getting work done. She couldn't afford a new car every four years like Keisha. There was a bus stop a few streets down from the diner but she didn't know what time the bus would arrive. She started on her stroll to the bus stop, hoping that the bus would have a working AC.

She was a half block away when the bus drove past her. She ran the rest of the way. She was the last to get on the bus when the smell of funk and heat mixed together hit her nostrils. She wanted to stop her breath but she couldn't. She was inhaling and exhaling faster than normal because of the sprint she did to get the bus. The entire bad odor made her wanted to throw up. Every stop the bus made a different funk entered.

She couldn't inhale this pollution any longer. Nikki exited the bus and dialed 411 for a number for a cab. She would have rather spent her last dime on a cab instead of being miserable on the bus. Nikki missed New York. She missed the days when she could flag down a dollar van.

Before Nikki got accepted at Saint Vincent Medical School she was running the street, partying, but never took it to the third degree like Keisha. Nikki's mother had passed away from a heart attack because she was yelling at her to change her life. Nikki promised herself that she would be a cardio surgeon so she could mend hearts. Her mother died of a broken heart because of her so mending hearts would help her forgive herself for her mother's death.

The taxi took less than ten minutes to rescue her from the hot sun. *Thank God this taxi has AC. But no thanks for the secondhand smoke.* After another ten minutes in the taxi Nikki paid her ten dollars and got out. She hastily passed the mailbox, heading for shelter, but made a U-turn because the mailbox was overflowing. She separated junk from bill as she walked from the mailbox.

"I would advise you to walk with your head above your shoulder, young lady."

The voice startled Nikki and the mail fell out of her hand. She held her head up only to see a tall, strong man with a strong, firm voice looking down at her. The man spoke with authority, which reminded her of Eddie Murphy's father in the movie *Coming to America.*

"I'm looking for Keisha. Is she home?"

"Are you her pimp? And do I look like Keisha's keeper?"

The man's jaw tightened and he wrinkled his brow. His forehead had many lines as if each line represented a year of his stressful life. She bent to pick up the mail off the ground and the man raised his voice to command respect as if he was a drill sergeant.

"If she is here I would advise you to go get her!"

She was taken aback by the tone in his voice. *Who the hell does he think he is?* "You need to lower your damn voice because I'm not your child."

"It's apparent that you don't know who I am."

"Enlighten me. Which one of her many men are you? Eric, Jerome . . ." Nikki walked passed him, still calling out random names, when the man roared like a lion.

"I am her father!"

Her eyes widened; her mouth fell open. Why didn't she see the resemblance? The similarities were all there; besides, he barked orders just like she would. How could she have known that Keisha had a father? Keisha never spoke of her family. It was as if she'd been raised by a pack of wild animals.

She felt so ashamed because she had called him a pervert. He stood still with both hands at his side, staring at her with intensity in his eyes. She apologized profusely because she had insulted him greatly.

"I'm Nikki, her roommate." She skeptically stretched her arm for a handshake, hoping to ease the tension, but her gesture was ignored. "Would you like to come inside?" She smiled, hoping that it would put him at ease, but instead he gave her a stern look proving that he was cold as ice, and her smile disappeared.

"Young lady, what are you doing with your life?"

"Well, I'm attending medical school to be a heart surgeon so when your daughter gives you a heart attack I'll be the one to save your life."

He didn't take that gesture lightly. His brow wrinkled even more.

Nikki was relieved and let out a sigh when she saw Keisha's car pull into the driveway. Keisha stepped out of her car, not caring to know who Nikki was speaking with. She grabbed her many shopping bags then slammed the door shut. She pointed her key forward and the well-polished and shiny black Benz answered with a beep. Her father's eyes widened when he saw his daughter he hadn't seen for years.

Keisha stopped when she turned and saw her father. "Daddy!" She released her shopping bags from her grip. Her phone and her keys fell out of her hand when she saw father. "Daddy!" The little girl inside her wanted to run to him. She took a couple steps forward then stopped herself.

It was a tense moment and Nikki was unsure about what she should do. She wanted to go inside but her feet wouldn't move. She stared at Keisha and for a quick second she saw fear in her eyes, but it was abruptly subdued by defiance.

"I hope you are doing something productive with your life like your roommate."

Keisha looked at Nikki with intense fury. Step-by-step Nikki slowly dismissed herself. This was a family affair and she didn't want to be a part of it or this family.

"Why the hell are you here? And how did you know where to find me?"

"You will not speak to me in that tone!" He stood directly in front of her and she took a couple of steps back. "Your mother is in the hospital worried about you. She needs you there with her."

"You took your head out your mistress's lap to come up for air but not long enough to realize that your wife needed you too?"

He slapped her face and she stumbled backward; luckily the car was there to break her fall.

As a child Keisha had witnessed her father putting his hands on her mother, the same way he had just put his hand on her. Realizing what he just did, he ran over to her but her stare was cold.

He held his head down in shame and turned his back to her. Tears welled up in his eyes. He was disappointed in himself. He had come to make things right with her, not worse. The army had taught him how to control his anger and how to be a man but he allowed his anger to get the best of him. She lashed out at him like a snake with a venomous tongue. Her cold words melted the ice around his heart and he felt her pain. He was no longer the iron man. Tears were now running down his face.

She knew he was now weak and she tore him to shreds with her words. "Where were you when my mother needed you?"

"I got reactivated in the army! When they call you have to go."

"The same old army excuse. Why didn't you die in the army?" she said with gritted teeth. She was heartless and cold.

He turned to face his daughter in disbelief. He fell to his knees, sobbing. "That was a long time ago and I am a better man now! I am a better man," he stated, pounding the ground with his fist, expressing his grief.

"If you consider killing people making you a better man, you are so deranged. You should have died in the army because you are dead to me!"

She walked past him drowning in his sorrow. She didn't have a soft spot for him. She wasn't touched by his performance. She stormed inside, instantly turning her fury on Nikki. "You and your damn goody-goody attitude. Do you have to parade that fact that you're going to school every chance you get?"

"He asked and I—"

"Try keeping your damn mouth shut next time." Keisha could cut down a tree with one lash from her tongue. Her father wasn't a role model himself. She caught him having an affair with his secretary but instead of ending it or admitting his fault, he would buy her silence with money, expensive presents, and shopping sprees with his mistress. She carried the guilt of betraying her mother throughout her young years. She despised her father and every man. She vowed to herself never to let them do to her what her father did to her mother. Her mother was also a weak woman who never stood up for herself. Keisha was disappointed in her mother for staying with her father and not divorcing his self-righteous ass. She also promised herself she would never be as weak as her mother.

Chapter 5

It was ten p.m. when Keisha finally finished perfecting herself. Keisha sprayed her Chanel perfume in the air, then turned around in a circle so each drop would hit her body softly. Keisha had a job to do and she had all the right skills for the position. Her uncle had promised her $5,000 and she wanted every penny of it, but she got a bigger thrill from thinking about her conquest tonight. She had the skills and the experience, but also a few extra qualities that would come in handy. Bling's show was scheduled to begin at twelve-thirty a.m. but she also had to go see Hype do his thing at another venue at eleven p.m. She had plenty of time to make it without rushing. She had told Tina to drive her own car just in case she was going to take her conquest home for some extra convincing.

She got to the club and was taken aback when she saw the long line outside. "I'm not standing in that long-ass line." She actually wished Tina had ridden with her because she would have had her bribe the guard with her number. With every step she took she was telling her feet not to fail her. She had extra-high heels besides her feet were already hurting. Keisha approached from the back of the line with no intention of joining.

"What's up, Keisha?" The security guard was an acquaintance of hers she knew from partying in Queens. He signaled for her to come up front. A few angry people hurled negative comment at her but she sashayed her way past them.

"Thanks, Jenkins."

"Anytime, Keesh."

"Still working in the Coliseum during the day?"

"You know it," he replied.

"I'll surprise you with lunch one of these days."

The club was already crowded, not to mention the people who were still waiting in line to come in. She spotted Tina at the bar and made her way over to her. Tina greeted her with an apple martini. Keisha felt piercing stares cutting her like a knife. She viewed her surroundings and noticed a few pointing fingers and rolling of the eyes. She was hated by many but she felt empowered because she was the center of attention. She was a trendsetter so females looked to her for what was in style. Females held their men tight because she was disrespectful enough to give her number to a man whether he was with his woman or not. She was not only presumptuous but confident.

A man and his woman gazed at her but they both stared for different reasons. Nevertheless, they stared. Keisha turned her head in their direction only to see the woman almost give herself whiplash; but the man winked at her. She blew him a kiss and his woman slapped his face. Two guys tried to engaged in a conversation but Keisha was not in the mood to be entertained by two broke-pocket men. Even though looks could be deceiving, Keisha knew how to tell real from the fake. It was a craft to her and she perfected it well. She could size them up by their fake brands and cheap cologne.

A group of men were escorted into the party and the females ran toward them but the bouncer held them at bay. One of the men went on stage and the females went wild.

Game on. Here we go; it's time to put operation seduction in motion.

"Come on, girl, let's get a closer view." Tina pulled her closer to the crowd. It wasn't her style to be a groupie but she figured she might as well get a better view. She made her way to the middle of the crowd, pushing past everyone with no apologies.

Hype had street swag. His musical style was a little Drake mixed with a little Kanye West: playful but cocky. The women were all swarming him like bees when he came off stage. The security escorted him to a private both as if he was big pimping.

"What a fucking joke. He's not even making real money yet. But how am I going to get to him?" *I could see if Tina can get in the VIP room, then have her tell him about me wanting to meet him. No. Tina might act a fool and create a mess; besides, I really don't want to spend my entire night with this young buck.*

"I got it! Jenkins. That's why sometimes times it's good to have friends in high and low places." She walked over to Jenkins, who was now standing guard by the room.

"You know that I can't let you in, Keisha." He shook his head.

"Come on. What about for a plate of fried chicken or some extra cash?"

"I'll take the money."

She went in her purse and slid a twenty in his pocket.

"Hype, I'm sending in another one!" he yelled over the music.

Keisha got behind the curtain and girls had their breasts out and were kissing each other for his satisfaction.

"Yes, yes. What do we have here?" he said, impressed by Keisha. "All of you can leave." He hurried them out of the room.

Keisha was disgusted by him but she had a job to do so she played the role.

"Since you interrupted my session you have to pick up where they left off." He reclined.

"Not so fast. Let me see what size you are working with because I definitely don't want to waste my time. Especially if you can't handle a woman like me." She knew that would have him cease his antics; besides, no man wants to be questioned about his size.

"I like a woman who takes charge. You're sexy and confident. I love you. Marry me." He took his diamond pinky ring off his finger and got down on his knee in front of her. Keisha knew she had him hook, line, and sinker.

When she got to the other club Bling was already on stage. Every desperate female was up front, trying to reach out and touch, except a few couples who remained at a distance. The videographer turned the camera toward the back and the bright light was blinding. But her pupils adjusted to the light and she refocused on Bling and his eyes focused on her because she definitely stood out from the rest.

He moved across the stage, serenading the females, but a magnetic force drew him back to her; he was captivated by her beauty. Keisha knew she had his attention so she walked away knowing his eyes were following her every move. Keisha made her way to the bar where she ordered another drink and watched the rest of his performance. After taking a few pictures with some of his fans, Bling made his way to the bar with his posse tagging along. One of his friends whispered in Keisha's ear but she showed no interest in what he had to say. She looked past him and addressed Bling. "I enjoyed your performance. You are very talented."

"Thanks."

"I see you have a lot of fans."

"Does that include you too?" He smiled at her.

"She is more like a groupie," the guy she had ignored stated for all to hear.

"So where is your next performance? I would like to check you out."

"Go check out my Facebook page. You will find upcoming events there, or you can follow me on Twitter."

He turned to walk away from her. She held on to his arm but he loosened her grip.

"Where are you rushing off to? I was hoping you wouldn't mind going somewhere quiet so we could talk. Maybe we can get out of here."

"I'm sorry to disappoint you but I have other engagements. Besides, I'm a married man." He turned away from her.

Her ego was shattered. Her heart skipped a beat. She was choking on her ego. She was about to faint. He turned her down. She swallowed her spit trying to push down her guts because they wanted to come up.

"Are you intimidated by the challenge?" she retorted.

"I won't refuse the offer; besides, there is nothing wrong with some groupie love. I can make you a star, a porn star!" They all laughed.

"Okay. I have a better offer. Let me sample the product and I can put you at the front of the line to get with my friend," the annoying friend added.

She looked at him as if he were an annoying barking poodle trying to get some attention. He continued laughing so hard and spilled his drink on her expensive Jimmy Choos. A few fans bum-rushed Bling, pushing Keisha out of the way. She was furious. She stormed into the bathroom irritably, grabbing paper towels and wiping her feet.

"Who the hell does he think he is turning me down? I'm the hottest chick in this bitch."

A few females entered the bathroom and she composed herself. They complimented her on her outfit, even her makeup.

"Wouldn't you like to be me?" she said, annoyed.

She grabbed her purse and exited the bathroom, annoyed by the females invading her space and informing her of what she already knew. This was the first time in her life she had ever been turned down by any man, whether he was gay or straight.

She left the club upset and angry that she had failed her mission. She didn't even bother to tell Tina that she was leaving. She took her shoes off in the car because the pain was more than she could bear.

She pulled into her driveway and exited her car, tiptoeing to the door. She turned the key in the door and remembered that she didn't secure her car. Beep, beep. The car answered when she pressed the lock button.

She launched her shoes into the wall, unleashing her anger. She planted her face into her pillow and screamed. When she picked her face up off the white pillowcase the outline of her face showed her true color. It was something out of a scary movie. She created perfection with her makeup but she was ugly on the inside. The pillowcase said it all.

She walked to the kitchen and poured herself a glass of red wine and drank it in one shot. Then she guzzled from the bottle, drowning her self-pity. The phone in the kitchen indicated she had new messages. She reached over with the bottle and pressed play.

"Hey, love," a baritone voice sang. "I'm in town and you know I want to see my number one girl."

She displayed a smile. The message was from a rich entrepreneur who would call her whenever he was in town. She didn't consider herself to be an escort but she always got a check for a large sum whenever he left. One of his many houses was in Connecticut and for however long he stayed Keisha would be wined and dined like a princess. Mr. Money was visiting his Connecticut home to see what changes he could make to make it more earth friendly. He was going green. He was also a health-conscious person and had stopped eating meat the last time she saw him but her meat was still on the menu if you know what I mean. Her confidence resurfaced and she danced to her bedroom. After all, her confidence was cracked, not shattered by Bling. Now it was a whole new ball game. She had to come up with a plan, a good plan, because she was going to attack with weapons of mass destruction. She turned the stained pillow to the opposite side and laid her head to rest with a smile on her face.

Chapter 6

The ringing of the phone woke Keisha from her slumber. She reached for her cell on the nightstand without turning her head. "Hello," she answered with a raspy voice.

"I miss you."

Keisha tossed the sheet from her body and sat up. "Martin?"

"Yes. It's me. I miss you, baby girl. I want you back in my life and just to prove how serious I am, there's a surprise outside for you."

Keisha wiped the crust out of her eyes and ran to the window and a brand new Benz sat in her driveway with a red bow. "Oh my God!" Keisha screamed.

Nikki ran out of her bedroom, thinking something was wrong. Keisha was jumping up and down on the couch like a madwoman.

"What the hell is your problem?" Nikki yelled at her.

Keisha grabbed her arm and brought her to the window. "Look! That's my new car."

Nikki walked away from her without rejoice. "As if you needed another car."

Keisha composed herself and brought her attention back to the phone. "Thanks, Martin."

"Don't worry about the payments. I got that. Can I see you tonight?"

"Not tonight, Martin. Besides, things have changed." Ever since his wife had found out about their affair she hadn't seen or heard from him. Keisha wasn't going to inquire about his wife or kids because she couldn't care less.

"I'm sorry for the way things ended but I'm going to make all that up to you. All the paper work is good on the car so you can start driving today."

If sugar daddy's intentions were to get back with her it wasn't going to happen. She would tell him whatever he wanted to hear to get what she wanted but honestly she wasn't interested in him anymore. "Bye, Martin." Keisha ended the conversation and ran to the shower. She wasn't going to waste her day inside when she had a new Benz to ride around in.

The bathroom was steamy when Nikki opened the door. She couldn't see herself in the mirror. She took a washcloth from the towel rack and defrosted the mirror. Keisha was singing in the shower so she didn't even realize that Nikki had entered. Nikki took her toothbrush from the holder and covered the bristles with Crest toothpaste. Keisha slid the shower curtain and almost gave herself a heart attack when she saw Nikki. Nikki continued brushing her teeth.

"I would appreciate some privacy," Keisha protested with water dripping from her naked body.

Nikki rinsed her mouth and looked at her from the mirror. "Do you mind stepping out the shower so I can get in?"

Keisha reached for her towel. "You better get down off your high horse before I push you off." Keisha walked out of the bathroom.

Nikki had an attitude when she saw Keisha's new car but it wasn't because she was jealous. It was simply because she opposed the lifestyle Keisha chose.

Keisha got dressed in record time. She ran outside and opened the door to her new Benz and inhaled the leather interior. She hastily walked to her five-year-old BMW to retrieve her CDs.

She pulled out of her driveway and slowly drove down the street with the red bow still on top of the car, letting everyone know that her ride was brand new. She was the envy of every woman. Just days ago Keisha was driving a five-year-old BMW and girls were envious.

Keisha approached a stoplight and pulled up next to a car carrying two men with their hormones raging. They were hooting and hollering. She blew them a kiss and they sped off with their manhood swollen big as their male egos.

Keisha didn't have a destination in mind. She would just drive wherever the wind blew. After an hour of driving she made an impromptu decision to get her hair done. She didn't have an appointment but her hairdresser, Poochie, would still take her because she was a big tipper. Keisha pulled up just in time to get a parking spot in front of the salon. A woman left the salon with a ghetto fabulous hairdo and Keisha busted out laughing. She was parked in front of the salon so Keisha took her spot.

She got out of her new Benz and all eyes were on her. She entered the salon and Poochie barked at her, "I know you are not coming in here without an appointment on a Saturday."

Keisha walked over and kissed her on her cheek. A customer was in her chair getting the last roller put in. "Come on, P. You know I'm going to tip you big."

Poochie called her next customer and started shampooing her hair. "I don't know, Keisha. I have three people ahead of you."

Keisha viewed the room for the first time and noticed all the chairs were occupied. "I just need a flat iron. It won't take long. Just tell one of these nappy-head chicks to wait."

Poochie rolled her eyes at her. "Don't come in here starting no shit. But I'll see if I can squeeze you in. If not you just have to let Toya do your hair."

"P. I'll pay you double."

Keisha looked over at Toya and rolled her eyes. This was the first time Poochie had rejected her money. *What the hell is that all about? Maybe that bitch is jealous of my new ride. No matter how many nappy roots you perm you can never be on my level. So go on, hater, continue to hate. I should just leave this raggedy-ass salon.* She was about to put one foot in front of the other but had second thoughts because nobody could do hair better than Poochie.

Keisha picked up a fashion magazine and sat in the empty shampoo chair. She skipped through several pages before the black Dolce & Gabbana dress caught her eyes. The dress looked better than the one David's ho for hire had on. It was knee length with low-cut cleavage with sheer lace down to the belly button. Keisha knew it would hug her body perfectly. *I have to get that.* She made a personal note to herself.

She was there for more than an hour before it was finally her turn. "Mrs. G. fell asleep so I can squeeze you in."

Keisha got up, taking the magazine with her. "You call this squeezing me in? I've been here over an hour."

Poochie had the hot iron in her hand. "Sit you ass in this chair so I can straighten your nappy roots."

Keisha's phone started to ring. She took a quick glance and it was Tina. She had forgotten that she was supposed to meet with her for lunch at their favorite Jamaican restaurant. She knew Tina well enough to know that her patience ran thin. Keisha checked her watch and she was more than a half hour late. She knew Tina would be furious. "Hello. Tina, I'll be there in a minute." She switched the cell phone to her left ear because Poochie threatened to burn her with the flat iron if she didn't keep still.

"Don't tell me you're getting your hair done and I'm here waiting on you."

"I'm not getting my hair done," Keisha lied.

Poochie looked her in the face. "You're going to hell in a hand basket," she whispered.

"I'll meet you there," Keisha said, covering her phone.

"May I take your order?" Keisha heard the waiter ask Tina. His accent was sharp but exotic to make you want him to read the whole menu out loud.

"It's a known fact that Jamaican men are wild beasts in the sheets," Keisha teased. "Besides, a one-night stand wouldn't hurt."

"Can you give me a few more minutes please?"

"Take your time."

"Keisha. You should see his thick, juicy lips. He is hot."

"Calm down. He can't look that good. I would have seen him already, as often as I dine there."

"If only I could see what his body looks like under his shirt."

"You need to dismiss the thought because you know he can't support you on a waiter's income. Unless you could deal with a broke stalker." They both laughed.

"But, damn, a one-night stand wouldn't hurt."

"Like I said, broke stalker. But I'll be there in a minute."

"You said the same thing ten minutes ago."

Keisha hung up the phone and got up out of the chair. "Here is fifty. Keep the change. Mrs. G, it's your turn," Keisha bellowed as she passed by her, waking her from her slumber.

Tina was calling her back and she ignored the call. Telling her she would be there in a minute wouldn't work this time. It took her twenty minutes to pull up at the restaurant. She saw Tina outside, looking up and down the street for any sign of her car. Keisha's phone was ringing again and she knew it was Tina calling her because she saw her with the phone at her ear. "Have some patience, woman." She took the keys out of the ignition.

"Where the hell are you? If you are not here in ten minutes I'm leaving."

Keisha exited her new candy-apple Benz and waved at her. Tina jaw dropped open. Cars slowed in both directions, giving her access to cross the street. She did her regular sassy walk as if she were on the runway. Tina hugged her, screaming with joy and envy.

"Why didn't you tell me that you bought a new car? You are such a bitch."

"I know."

The bystanders commented on her car, also about her, and she loved it. They walked into the restaurant like two peas in a pod. Tina's six-inch heel broke, causing her to trip, falling into the arms of a man with unpleasantly smelly armpits.

"Are you irie, sista?"

Holding her breath she nodded her head because she didn't dare to inhale his polluted odor.

"It's fate dat brought us togeda."

"It is I who broke us apart." She pushed him away from her and departed from him.

The waiter strolled to their table with a wide smile on his face showing off his pearly white teeth. This time Tina was ready to order. She knew exactly what she wanted and it was him. "Are you ready to order now, miss?"

"Do you have a twin? You are the exact replica of someone I know," Keisha chimed in. "I see good looks run in the family."

The waiter smiled at the compliment. "Are you ladies ready to order?"

Tina opened her mouth to speak but Keisha cut her off. "Are you on the menu?"

"It depends on what the order is."

Tina was looking at Keisha, unsure of her intentions. "I'm ready to . . ." Tina tried to speak again, but before she could finish Keisha cut her off in midsentence and placed her order.

"I would like to have you on a silver platter." Keisha was going in for the kill. She questioned him about himself as if he were on the menu. The couple sitting at the table next to her was astonished at her bold pursuit. She told him what she wanted and laid down the rules of engagement. It was a one-time deal but if his performance was up to standards there was a possibility she would keep him around.

"I would love to take you on a tour of the kitchen. My shift is ending."

He was up for the tryst. Tina was baffled as to why Keisha would do that to her. She didn't think she would want to mingle with grease and pots and other utensils.

The waiter extended his arm to Keisha and she reached for it. "I'll let you know what the rock is cooking," Keisha stated as she left the table.

They entered the kitchen and the heat was the first thing to greet her, followed by all the different aromas of Caribbean cuisine. Two cooks took their attention away from the big pots and greeted the waiter with a respectful nod, while another placed chicken in a big pan of hot oil. She held his hand tight because she felt out of place.

"Can't stand the heat in the kitchen?" he whispered in her ear.

The warm air tickled her ear, sending signals to her breasts, arousing her nipples. They made a few turns and came to a red door at the end of the hall that denied any further access to anyone without a key. He reached in his pocket and took out a single key with a map of Jamaica hanging from it. He pushed the door open and the air-conditioned room was just what she needed. The room was an office. There was a desk with a computer and lots of receipts. There was a stereo playing a song by Beres Hammond. The walls were decorated by paintings representing the islands and there was also a couch with a jacket lying on it.

The waiter slowly removed his shirt as he danced to the music, revealing his chiseled chest with a few strands of hair growing from it. Keisha braced herself against the door because she could no longer feel the air from the air conditioner; her body was getting hot. He took her by the arm and brought her close to him and kissed her lips. His lips were soft and she was enjoying it. Her nipples hardened as he unbuttoned her shirt and his big hands cupped her breasts while his lips were still glued to hers.

He lifted her up, placing her on the desk. He unhooked her bra and his warm tongue met her already-hardened nipples, sending shivers down her spine. He slowly slid down her body like a snake, lifting her dress and taking her panties off with his teeth. His tongue greeted her candy pot and she held on to his head, relaxed her muscles and let her juices flow. Her legs trembled and he knew she was near her climax. He lifted his head up and she tried to bring him back to her spot. She bit on her lips to make sure that this wasn't a dream.

The waiter unbuckled his belt and his pants fell to the ground. Keisha sat up and kissed his chest. He wasn't interested in what she could do for him. He was going to show her what he was more than capable of doing to her. He spun her around, bending her over so her ass would poke out at him. He kissed both cheeks and parted her legs. He fed her his manhood and she expressed what she felt with a deep moan. He covered her mouth and fed her more. He was enjoying her as much as she was enjoying him.

Keisha was close to her climax again when he stopped his motion and led her over to the couch and instructed her to get on top. She rode him to the beat of the reggae music playing on the stereo. The pleasure was intense. She was savoring the moment, trying to hold back her climax, until he reached up and squeezed her nipples. Her moans got louder and she went faster.

"Not yet; what's the rush?" He picked her up, taking her back to the desk, and placed her on her back. He gave her all of him and she wrapped her legs around his waist and dug her nails into his back. Keisha got to her climax and let out a scream that would break any glass in sight. The waiter was right there with her. He gathered all his energy, giving her all he got. He roared like a lion because he was the king of this jungle. He enjoyed every moment of it just like she did.

She lay there in amazement. She was satisfied. The thought of how she had just betrayed her friend didn't even cross her mind. She refreshed her makeup and reapplied her lip gloss. Piece by piece she picked up her clothes and dressed herself. Her eyes strayed to a few certificates on the wall behind the desk and saw the name Damien Harvey: the owner. She smiled from ear to ear then finished getting dressed.

She blew him a kiss as she left his office, leaving him still breathless on the couch. She composed herself as she took the walk of shame through the kitchen. Actually there was no shame in her game because Damien was the owner, not a broke-pocket waiter. The cooks stared with smile on their faces, knowing she had sampled the main course.

Chapter 7

Keisha raised her wrist, checking the time on her Gucci watch. It was 3:55. Her session with Damien had lasted over an hour. She swiftly made her way out the side exit, not wanting to deal with Tina just in case she was still waiting inside.

"Hell no!" Keisha bellowed, seeing the word BITCH stretched across her car in bold letters. She knew exactly who did it and she was going to deal with Tina. "I can't believe this jealous bitch did this to my car."

She pressed the send on her phone and redialed the last number that had called her. But Tina didn't answer; her call was forwarded to voicemail. "If you see me on the street, run, because I'm running your ass over."

Keisha sped off in a hurry to get to Tina's house. She went through a few yellow lights and ignored a few NO TURN ON RED signs. She made it to Tina's apartment but she didn't see her car in the driveway. She put her car in park and got out like a madwoman, leaving her door open. She ran up the stairs to apartment 119 and pounded the door like she was beating a drum.

"I know you are in there! Open the door before I kick it in. You think if you park around the block I wouldn't see your car?" Keisha didn't actually see Tina's car but she was hoping that would get her attention. "Your windows will be in pieces, bitch!"

Keisha ran down the stairs and hid herself at the side of the building. Tina came storming out of the apartment, and Keisha grabbed her and began pounding into her body as if her arms were a sledgehammer trying to break bricks.

"Get off me! Tina hollered. Keisha was still pounding her into the ground. This wasn't the projects so nobody was forming a circle around them. There was no cheering them on. No one even came outside to enjoy the wrestling match.

Keisha was in a rage. She felt two strong arms hoisting her off Tina. "Get the fuck off me!" She turned and faced two police officers, with the big, stocky officer still holding her arm.

"I should lock you both up for disturbing the peace!" He freed Keisha's arm.

"You should lock her up for destroying my car."

The officer looked at Tina.

"If anybody should be pressing charges it's me," Tina stated in her defense.

"You keyed my damn car, bitch!"

"Do either one of you want to press charges?"

"I do want to press charges. She destroyed my car."

The officer looked at Keisha. "She could also press charges for assault and battery. So, again, do either of you want to press charges?" They both remained quiet. "I didn't think so," the officer said.

Keisha waked off to her car and Tina climbed the stairs to her apartment. The officers watched Keisha until she was in her car. Keisha started her car and buckled her seat belt and drove off slowly. She had avoided going to jail and she was going to avoid a speeding ticket.

She got to her house just in time to see the UPS driver walking back to the truck. She honked on her horn and got his attention. She'd lost track of the time. She was expecting a delivery at 4:30 p.m. She signed and retrieved her package. She was excited like a kid in a candy store.

She ripped the box open and gold high-heel pumps presented themselves. She screamed in excitement as she took them out of the box. Her gold Jimmy Choos would complement her dress tonight. She placed her feet in her heels and they were a perfect fit.

Mark stood at the car door because she unknowingly left the door open. She saw the reflection and thought it was Nikki. "Aren't you jealous?" She kept her eyes down on her feet.

"I'm definitely not," the person stated in a deep voice.

She raised her head, startled to see Mark standing there, but, nevertheless, she modeled her shoes and Mark clapped in approval. Keisha led him in to the living room just like she did the first day he came to fix the cable. She sat on the couch and seductively crossing her legs.

"Is Nikki home? Can you tell her I'm here?"

His question and request went unanswered. "I met your twin today. I wonder if you guys have everything in common." Keisha went to sit next to him.

Mark instantly got up when Keisha came over and sat next to him. "What are you doing? You know I'm trying to be with Nikki. Is she here?"

Keisha walked over to him. "Are you scared? Don't tell me you have no self control."

Mark proceeded to the door. "Tell Nikki I brought lunch but she wasn't home."

Keisha took a hold of his shirt and pulled him back. "Calm down. I was just testing you. Sit. You don't want me to tell Nikki how rude you were to her roommate." Mark returned to take a seat on the couch. "Good boy. I'll bring this food to the kitchen. I'll be right back."

She walked to the kitchen and tossed the food on the table. She took down two wine glasses and filled them with red wine and walked back to the living room.

"I just spoke to Nikki; she is on her way. I always have a drink around this time so I figure you should have one to loosen you up. You seem a little tense. I won't bite." She handed the glass to him and sat next to him. Mark moved up from her. He took a big gulp from his glass and some spilled on his shirt. He got up and tried brushing it off.

"Oh my, you stained your shit." She took the glass from him and placed it on the coffee table. She returned her attention to his shirt. "Let me get the stain out for you."

He backed away from her. "It's okay. This was an old shirt. Don't worry about it."

Keisha was persistent. "I have a stain remover that does a good job. Trust me." She unbuttoned his shirt one button at a time, revealing his six pack. She was fascinated. Mark released the shirt from his back into her hand.

"You bitch!" Nikki yelled.

"I can explain." Mark stumbled on his words. Keisha had a big smile on her face. She turned her face, trying to hide her laugh. "I spilled and she—"

"Get the hell out!"

"Please let me explain," Mark begged.

"Leave!"

Mark hurriedly put his shirt on and embarrassingly escorted himself to the door.

"Before you start to pass judgments and act like a madwoman, let me clear up what just happened," Keisha brought herself to say.

"He's interested in me and not you so you throw yourself at him. Is that it?"

Keisha gave her a "bitch, please" look and took up both glass and headed to the kitchen, but Nikki was right behind her. "He's a cable guy. My aim is much higher. He's more your speed so let me nip this in the bud before your ass ends up homeless tonight. He brought you some lunch. I offered him a drink of wine. He spilled it on his shirt. I told him to take his shirt off so I could get the stain out and that's when you walked in. The man is innocent, Nikki."

Why am I tripping? I seriously don't think that Mark is Keisha's type even though she's a bitch. I will give her the benefit of a doubt. But why the hell am I acting jealous anyway? I'm not even dating this man. "What am I doing? I'm sorry for blowing up at you like that. I don't know what came over me."

"All is forgiven. That is to be expected from a woman who is falling in love."

"Who said anything about love?"

"You don't have to. It's written all over your face." Keisha pointed her finger at Nikki. "It says, 'love, love, love, and crazy love.'"

Nikki untied the bag with her lunch, revealing a chicken salad. She smiled because that's what she had ordered at the diner when she made a fool of herself the same way she just did.

Keisha walked away, still wearing her Jimmy Choos. They had arrived just in time for her to wear to the club tonight. This would be her second attempt to reel Bling in. Regardless if he was married she would do whatever she had to for him to sign to her uncle's label; besides, her $5,000 cash was worth it.

The doorbell chimed and she placed her shoes back in the box. *Who could this be?* The doorbell rang nonstop as if she had someone's husband in her condo. *Maybe that's Martin wife coming for the keys to the new car he bought me.*

Keisha reminisced on Martin being her sex slave. It was never boring with Martin. He liked to role play and he would always like to be treated like an animal. He liked to be tied up like a dog and told what to do. One of his specialties was to have Keisha take off her panties and toss them across the room. He would get down on all fours and crawled across the room, sniffing her panties, then pick them up with his teeth and carry them back to her. He would roll over on his back with his feet in the air when it was time for a treat. She would get down on all fours and he would crawl up behind her, then enjoyed her body like a doggie biscuit.

She lazily walked to the door, uninterested in another confrontation with another bitter wife, but she wouldn't hesitate to put a fist to her face. She opened the door and regretted not looking through the peephole first. Johnny stood there with a bunch of roses. She wanted to close the door but it was too late.

Johnny was a Jamaican guy from her old neighborhood who she dated when they were teenagers. He was persistent and presumptuous and also demanding. Johnny wanted to pick up where they left off from in their teenage years but she now enjoyed the fast life and had no intention of falling in love again or anytime soon. She made the biggest mistake when she ran into Johnny and invited him to her condo to chitchat, trying to find out how deep his pocket was. She found out that his wife ran off with his friend and emptied his bank account, leaving him penniless. Ever since that day he popped up whenever he felt like. He had no fashion sense, as if his wife took that, too. Keisha found ways to use him to her advantage. She turned him into her errand boy. He was always trying to impress her, but poor Johnny—emphasis on the word poor—he didn't stand a chance. Johnny was like a song you hated but when it came on you listened to it because you weren't close enough to the player to skip it. He liked to talk a lot about everything and anything. To someone who didn't know him, they would think he lived a great life once upon a time. Every other day it was a different story why he was broke. His most famous one of all was that he was one of the people who got caught in the Bernie Madoff scheme.

"I was just on my way out to run some errands." Keisha politely took the roses from Johnny.

"I'll take you wherever your heart desires."

She wouldn't be caught dead in that old, beat-up car. "No, thank you. Today is a busy day for me but thanks for the flowers. I'll put these in some water before they wither." She walked away from the door. She couldn't cope with his stories today.

She entered the kitchen and tossed the roses on the table. She opened the cabinet and reached up to get a crystal vase that she had previously gotten from Johnny. Johnny crept up behind her, grabbing her around the waist. The vase fell out of her hand, hitting the floor and smashing into little pieces, just like her disheveled life.

"You almost gave me a heart attack!"

"That's not what I want to attack."

"If it weren't for your cheap cologne, I wouldn't know it was you. You are definitely wearing out your welcome."

Johnny wore a big smile on his face as he picked up the pieces of broken glass from the floor. She handed him the broom, disgusted by Johnny's presence. She took the roses and tossed them into the trash.

"I brought you roses and you throw them into the garbage!" Johnny spoke with rage in his voice.

"Would you rather I toss you in there instead?"

"When are you going to give me the chance to treat you like a lady so you can have my babies?" he pled desperately.

She had a sickened look on her face as she thought, *I really need to put Johnny in his place. He is my errand boy, my go-fetch boy. He walks into my house as if he is somebody. I'll knock him back to wherever the hell he came from if he don't leave me alone. Picture me having*

his babies, some filthy rug rats. The thought makes me
want to puke.

"You need to leave my apartment right now because
your cheap cologne is stinking up the room. Not to mention you have no money and it's making me nauseous.
Don't you have anything else to do with your time? Time
is like money; go spend it wisely."

He released the broom from his hand and it fell to the
floor. He walked out of the kitchen with his feelings hurt.
He got to the front door and Nikki was there with her keys
in her hand. Johnny pushed past her, almost knocking
her down.

"What a joke. Before I marry a man without any money
I'll commit myself to the psycho ward." Keisha swept the
broken pieces of glass into the dust pan. "Right now this
devil needs to wear Prada and he certainly can't afford it."

Keisha was all about money and vanity. Nothing else
mattered to her. Her motto for life was like the 50 Cent
album *Get Rich or Die Tryin'*, but the only difference was
she didn't want to work for it. Her beauty was a blessing
from God and she insisted to use it to her advantage.

Chapter 8

"I'm making a run to the store. Do you want me to pick you up anything?" Nikki asked, standing by Keisha's door.

"Yes. Pick me up some apples. You know, the dark red ones."

"I think the proper name is Red Delicious."

"I'll call it whatever the hell I want to call it." Nikki removed herself while Keisha was still yapping. "You always have to correct someone like you are so proper. Bitch, you are a damn improper fraction."

Nikki descended the steps. She would hardly waste her time fighting with Keisha. She knew Keisha had problems and issues that ran deep. All that acting tough was just a cover-up for her insecurities and to hide her fears. She was going to ask if she could use her car but she realized it wasn't a good idea, because she had just gotten her upset; and, besides, for every good deed Keisha did she would always need a bigger favor in return.

Nikki decided to walk the ten blocks to the grocery store. That was a bad idea. The white cotton leggings were baking her legs. Not to mention all the unwanted attention and compliments about her ass. The pink tank top clung to her breasts, defining her shape. She didn't have to worry about her feet hurting because her white Polo sneakers were comfortable.

The temperature seemed as if it had dropped because a sudden breeze rid her body of the perspiration that was forming on her nose. After five blocks Nikki felt as if she had been walking for days. She made a detour, walking another five blocks to the park to clear her head instead of to the grocery store.

She was out of breath when she finally made it to the park. She sat on a bench at the entrance and viewed the beauty of Mother Nature. It was still too hot outside for her liking but she was enjoying the beautiful scenery. The ocean spread wide in front of her with waves crashing against the sand. She wouldn't dare take a swim but from a distance the water looked inviting. If you looked out in the distance you could see waterfront houses, mansions you'd dream of one day living in with your husband and kids. The thought of Mark danced across her mind more often than she would have liked to admit.

She shook her head, trying to dismiss the thought. She got up, and started walking closer to the beach. In the distance she saw the silhouette of a shirtless man running in her direction. She was anxious to get closer because a better view of this perfectly shaped body would definitely get her mind off Mark. As she got closer she could see a six pack. The man wore sunglasses and a baseball cap so it was hard to recognize his face. Sweat ran down his chiseled, hairless chest. Mark was no longer on her mind. She replaced any thought she had about Mark with this picture-perfect man she now would fantasize about.

He ran past her and Nikki managed to hold her composure, even though she wanted to reach out and touch him. She turned her head to view his figure but her eyes were fixated on his body. She could not take her eyes away. The man turned and came running back in her direction. "I hope he didn't see me looking at him."

The man ran to her and ran circles around her.

"What the hell do you think you are doing?" She tried passing him again but he blocked her from getting by him. She was now annoyed by this man. "I have Mace and I'm not afraid to use it." She walked around him, and he held her arm, but she quickly pulled away then kicked him in the groin. He held on to his crotch and let out a painful moan. She was about to let him have another one but held her leg back when he called out her name. She didn't recognize the man standing in front of her. He took his shades off and she was amazed.

"Mark!"

She couldn't believe that this perfect body belonged to Mark. Nikki jogged here all the time and never ran into him before. *Could he be stalking me? Why is it that he shows up wherever I go?* Mark took a few agonizing steps and sat on a bench located to his right. "How is it that you always know my location?"

"This is a public park. I should be filing sexual harassment charges against you."

"You are the one exposing yourself by showing off your sweaty muscles and strong arms, not to mention your six pack."

Nikki was unconsciously describing everything she liked about his body. She couldn't believe this man was really Mark. His body was of an ancient God you read about. All this time, he had been hiding this perfectly sculpted body under his hideous work uniform.

A smile appeared on Mark's face, erasing the pain he was feeling, because he now knew that she was infatuated with his body. He started to flex his muscles, showing off even more. Nikki was tempted to touch but she fought back the urges to caress this body of a stallion.

"You are pathetic," she said defensively.

"Can this pathetic man take you to dinner tonight?"

"Maybe I should take you up on that offer to see if you can actually be a gentleman."

Mark smiled. "I would love to see if you can actually stop being a pit bull and let me treat you like a lady. How about I pick you up at seven?"

"No. Be there at eight and don't be late."

She walked away off from him and he watched her disappear in the distance just like he did the first time he saw her.

Chapter 9

Nikki got home and went straight to the shower, stripping down to her naked body. For once in a long time her mind wasn't on her books, but on Mark. She stood in the shower and the water beat on her 130-pound body's frame, loosening her muscles that were so tense from holding her composure when she stood in front of Mark. She wanted to touch his chest. She wanted to wrap her arms around him and get soaked in his sweat but she wasn't going to give in, not now. Nikki wanted to know more about him. She wanted to make sure that they were on the same page about what they both were looking for in a relationship, because she wasn't interested in a one-night stand.

Nikki hadn't been out in a long time so she had no idea what she would wear. She went through her entire closet, tossing clothes on her bed, and nothing seemed right for the occasion. She decided to take a stroll in Keisha's closet before she got home.

The long walk-in closet was color coordinated and well organized. It was as if Nikki was at an upscale store. Designer tags hung from most of the garments. Nikki was lost into a world of fashion she knew nothing about. Nikki didn't want to stand out too much so she opted for a black dress.

She hurried back to her bedroom and was shocked to see the time. "Oh shit. It's after seven and my hair isn't done." Her phone started ringing and she was in a panic.

"I hope that's not Mark saying he's outside." She looked at the caller ID and it was him. "Why is he calling? I hope he's not cancelling on me."

She answered, trying to act coy. "Hello."

Mark cleared his throat before speaking. "I'm just confirming our date at eight."

Nikki breathed a sigh of relief. She was honestly looking forward to the date and was actually glad that he didn't cancel. "Yes, we are still on. Bye, Mark." She quickly hung up the phone because she needed all the time to beautify herself; besides, she wanted to be out of the house before Keisha got home and caught her wearing her dress.

"Straight or curly?" Nikki was unsure of how she wanted to wear her hair. "I'll just leave it straight."

Nikki ran to the bathroom to plug in the flat iron to give it a once-over. It was much quicker to straighten than curl. While the iron got hot she did her makeup. She applied a face powder with some mascara. She also tweezed the new growth out of her eyebrows. She added lip gloss to her lips and that's all she had time to do. "Less is more, especially now." She puckered her lips, giving herself a kiss.

Her hair took less time than she had thought. All this rushing was making her sweaty. She took a deep breath and calmed herself down. Nikki finished getting dressed and impatiently waited for Mark with time to spare. Every car that drove by she nervously looked out the window at, hoping it wasn't Keisha.

"Where the hell is he?" She didn't want to call Mark to seem too anxious so she paced back and forth to calm her nerves. Nikki checked the time and it was 7:59 p.m. He wasn't late so she couldn't be mad at him but she wished he was actually early.

The horn sounded and Nikki opened the door and went outside without the usual ritual of having the man wait an extra five minutes.

Nikki didn't have any decision in picking the restaurant. Mark wanted to surprise her and prove that he was a man of substance. They drove for twenty minutes on I-95 South, getting off at exit eight in Stamford, Connecticut. Nikki was wide-eyed when they pulled up at the Marriott Hotel. "What the hell are we doing here?"

Mark laughed out loud. "Relax. It's not what you think."

The valet opened Nikki's door and she hesitated to get out.

"Mark, I'm not getting out of this car."

Mark got around to her door and stretched out his hand for her to take. "It's not what you think, I promise."

Nikki got out of the car without taking his hand. Mark led the way inside and approached the elevator. Nikki had her arms crossed walking next to him. The elevator door opened and they got in. Mark pressed the tenth-floor button. And Nikki looked at him suspiciously. Mark tried to hold her hand but she resisted.

The elevator door opened up to an exquisite restaurant. The setting was beautiful. There was a piano in the center of the circular restaurant. Nikki was amazed. He reached for her hand but this time she didn't resist. They were escorted to a table for two and were immediately served complimentary champagne.

"I'm amazed" Nikki said, relieved that Mark wasn't presumptuous enough to take her to a hotel and order room service and think that was classified as a date.

"I'm not as shallow as you think," Mark retorted.

Nikki was facing the door when she was seated and noticed she was now facing the bar. She now wore a puzzled look on her face. Mark smiled, noticing her curiosity.

"Are we moving?" Nikki questioned.

"Yes, we are." The restaurant rotated 360 degrees, which overlooked a small part of the city.

"I have to admit that this is exquisite."

"I have to admit that you look very exquisite also."

"You're not looking too shabby yourself. I must say you dust off pretty well."

"So what time is your curfew? I know mother hen is at home waiting with an iron belt."

Nikki was reluctant to laugh at Mark's joke but Mark made a funny face imitating a fish, which caused her to laugh out loud. A couple dining next to them glared over at her and she sipped on her glass of Pinot Grigio white wine. Mark gazed at her intently because her smile was beautiful, which made her more attractive. He was impressed with the way she carried herself. Her poise and her elegance were rarities in women nowadays.

"You have a beautiful smile. You should flaunt it more often."

"I will, when a joke is worthy of a laugh."

They laughed and talked without an awkward moment. Mark was quite intelligent, despite Nikki's stereotypical thinking of him. Surprisingly Nikki was letting down her guard; it was apparent that she was going to let him into her life.

"So tell me something interesting about yourself, Miss Nikki."

She had just put a piece of red velvet cake in her mouth and couldn't speak at that moment. *So for the past hour we've been talking he's found nothing interesting about me? Was Keisha right? Am I really that boring?* She swallowed without fully chewing. "How about you tell something about yourself? Starting with your last name." She raised the fork and put the last piece of cake into her mouth.

"Gray," Mark said proudly.

It was a name with no substance but she pictured herself wearing it proudly: Mrs. Shavelle Gray. It would roll off her tongue gracefully. Nicolette was her middle name, hence the nickname Nikki.

"Did I mention that I have a degree in business management?"

With that, Mark had put the icing on the cake. Nikki's eyes widened. "So why are you fixing cable?" she said without hesitation.

"It's paying the bills right now."

She was impressed by the fact that he had a degree. The waiter came with the check and like a gentleman Mark picked up the tab. Nikki got up off her chair, revealing her naked back. She walked in front of Mark and he was hypnotized by her figure. The dress clung to her body, outlining every curve. Her four-inch heels elongated her legs. She was about five feet four inches tall and she had a sexy walk to match her attitude.

She was almost at the door when she tripped over the unlevel carpet on the floor. Mark caught her, breaking her fall a couple of feet from the ground. He held her in his arms and stared into her eyes. Her heart skipped a beat. He went in for a kiss.

"I can't," she stopped him.

"I'm sorry. I didn't mean to."

"Don't apologize; you did nothing wrong. I just can't kiss you in this uncomfortable backbreaking position."

"I'm so sorry."

"There you go again apologizing." She adjusted her posture.

"I'm sor—"

"Shut up and kiss me."

The kiss was sensual. It was all that she expected it to be and more. Nikki was the aggressor. She led and Mark followed. They forgot that they were still at the restaurant until a gentleman standing behind them with his wife wanting to get by cleared his throat. She embarrassingly fixed her hair and got out of the way. They held hands and left the restaurant to Mark's car.

Mark opened her door like a gentleman. She got in then leaned over, opening his door. That was one of the oldest tests of all time, to see if the lady would open the man's door after he opened hers. He got in the driver seat and gave her a look of approval. She rolled her eyes because she couldn't believe he tried to test her in such a predictable way.

He wasn't ready to end the night just yet so he convinced her to go for a drink at the new sports bar downtown. Going to a bar wasn't something she wanted to do. She would have rather been home with her books, but because the night was going so great she didn't want to ruin it.

"A little Hennessy and Coke won't hurt."

"What?" Her words had surprised him. "You know damn well you can't handle that."

"There is a lot you don't know about me, Mr. Gray."

They arrived at the sports bar downtown and Nikki was a little tense. She had agreed to go but she hadn't done the bar-and-party scene in so long she felt out of place and overdressed. They went inside and it was way beyond her expectation. There wasn't the regular peanut eating, or drunken men screaming at the TV when their team was losing. This setup was different. The bar had its own section and then there were single booths for private conversations with their own flat-screen TVs.

"What will it be?" the waiter asked.

"I'll have a beer but this young lady will like a shot of Hennessy."

"Make that Hennessy and Coke. Thank you," Nikki corrected the order.

"I'll take that shot since she's a punk."

"It's coming right up." The waiter left them to their privacy.

A song by Drake was now playing: "I better find you loving. I better find your heart." Mark sang aloud, looking into her eyes. "So are you going to let me find your heart? I know you are hiding it somewhere in there."

"How about if you find my heart it's yours to keep?"

"Well, I'll start searching starting now."

The waiter returned with their drinks and Mark took the shot to his head. Nikki sipped her drink and it was straight Hennessy without the Coke. It burned her throat like hot tea. Nikki didn't make a fuss about her drink; she drank it like a man. *What the hell am I trying to prove drinking this shit? I can already feel it soaking in my body. Oh, God, he is fine. I haven't been with a man in a long time and if I finish this devil's piss I know he's going to be my second round of dessert.*

Nikki had been very flirtatious and Mark was surprised to see this side of her. "I see that your glass is empty. Do you need a refill?" he asked.

Nikki gazed down at the glass in her hand and it was surprisingly empty but she giggled like a schoolgirl. Her eyes were no longer bright-eyed and alert. They were now half closed and winking at Mark.

"Fill my cup and let it overflow," she said, stretching over the table to get closer to his face. He leaned in to greet her lips with his but she pulled herself back. "Not so fast. My kisses don't come cheap."

"What must I do to get a taste of those lips again?"

"'Put a ring on it.'" She reenacted the moves from the Beyoncé video.

"I might just do that."

The ride home was all laughter. Mark looked at her with lust in his eyes. Nikki had transformed into a new person. They pulled up in front of the house and the automatic light brightened the entrance to the house, indicating that someone was present. Keisha exited the house looking fashionable from head to toe.

"Come on, let's go anywhere but here. The night is still young." Nikki was having such a good time she had forgotten that she was wearing Keisha's dress.

"Sounds good to me!" Mark was gleeful. But before he could put his foot on the gas pedal a car pulled in front of them with its high-beam lights almost blinding them. Nikki shielded her eyes with her hand. Johnny exited the car and Keisha was livid.

"What are you doing here?" she snapped at him in an irritable tone.

Johnny wasn't dressed in his normal attire. His look was definitely an upgrade. He had a dapper look as if he could be on a runway. Keisha walked toward him and smelled the scent of his cologne; it was a high-end brand.

"I'm here to take you out, my lady." Johnny got down on one knee as if proposing marriage.

"Do I look like I want to be seen out in public with you?"

She walked away from him. It was evident that he was hurt by her statement. He yelled at her with anger in his voice. "Why the hell am I always trying to impress you?"

"Why are you, when the truth remains that you have no money so no matter how hard you try you will never have me in your bed?"

"I can't have you but anybody with money is always welcome in your bed."

"That's right. Are you jealous?"

"It really seems like everybody can get a slice of you but you're acting like you don't want me. You're really the bitch everybody says you are. How much money do you want to sleep with me? On second thought I don't even want you anymore because I don't buy from the sale rack and you are definitely on sale."

"Even on the sale rack you can't afford me!"

Mark quickly exited his car because he knew the argument wasn't going to end well. "It's obvious that the lady isn't interested. So be a gentleman and leave her alone."

Why the hell did he have to be captain save a ho? Now I have to get out this damn car and have Keisha eat me alive for taking her dress. Well it's time to go face the music.

Keisha had a look of shock on her face, as if she was surprised to see Nikki and Mark together. Johnny stared at Keisha with a look of revulsion in his eyes. All the love he had for her had gone. His piercing eyes demolished the high pedestal he had put her on. She was now a repulsive rodent to him.

"You will regret this night," he stated as he walked back to his car.

Keisha looked at Nikki, then at Mark, searching for an answer as to where they were coming from. She was more interested in where they were coming from than in anything Johnny had to say. "You need to take my dress off before you ruin it. Brands don't look right on you. Stick to the cheap knockoffs you're used to. And the next time you decide to borrow my damn dress, ask me first." She got into her car and drove off.

Chapter 10

Keisha was steaming with anger. All the insults Johnny had thrown her way had made her miserable because of all the things she wished she would have said to Johnny but didn't. After twenty minutes of driving Keisha got to the club and it was unusually hot inside, or maybe it was just her. She immediately made her way to the bathroom and freshened up her makeup. Minutes later she parted through a crowd of groupies waiting for Bling to grace the stage. She went straight to the bar and ordered a Red Bull. The waitress placed the Red Bull on the counter.

"Drinking out of a can is not my style." Keisha was being a diva.

The waitress looked at her, rolling her eyes. "And your point is?"

Keisha exhaled aloud. "Your job is to pour it into a glass. Do I need to tell you how to do your job?"

The bartender slid the glass to her. "Pour it your damn self." The bartender walked to the opposite end of the bar.

The crowd went wild chanting Bling's name as he went on stage, but she held her composure. She would be calm, cool, and collected. Tonight she would reside at the bar and the prey would come to her, because every hunter knows that a thirsty animal always finds a water hole. There was no denying Bling's talent. He was reggae with a little R&B flava.

"Girl, I want you inna mi life. I want you to be mi wife."

The crowd went wild as if his words were personally addressed to them. The bouncers were trying to hold the groupies at bay as Bling serenaded the crowd. He was dodging undergarments as if they were bullets being thrown at him. "Girls mi love unuh." He exited the stage for another artist to serenade the pack of wild beasts that wanted to devour him. A groupie sneakily tried to go backstage. She was embarrassingly carried out by two bouncers. One bouncer held her arm and the other held her legs. Her crotch was exposed for all to see. A few horny bastards took the opportunity to reach out and touch.

"Let go off of me!" the girl screamed.

"Get your nasty ass out of here," the bouncer who was holding her arms retorted. The other bouncer was getting a free peep show.

With all this pandemonium going on, I hope he doesn't sneak out the back door. Keisha drank her Red Bull from a glass with a straw as she tried to stay calm.

"Are you trying to get with Bling, too?"

The voice startled Keisha a she spun around the barstool to see Mark. "What are you doing here?"

"So now I have to report to you like your friend Nikki?"

Keisha spun around, facing the direction Bling should have been coming from. *I hope he doesn't come out now. Mark standing here will ruin everything. I have to get rid of his ass.* "Speaking of Nikki, does she know that you are at a bar trying to pick up a one-night stand because she won't give you any loving? Well, I'm assuming she didn't." Keisha searched his eyes for an answer but he walked away with a sarcastic smile.

Keisha was glad he left but the question was unanswered. She wanted to know the answer but she knew Nikki wouldn't tell her. Keisha was getting up to go after him but the sudden outburst of screams caught her attention. The bouncers were guiding Bling to the bar. *I wish I had time to reapply my damn lip gloss.* She sipped from the glass, trying to calm her nerves. "I wish I had a stronger drink."

Bling's eyes widened when he saw Keisha sitting at the bar. The dress she had on would make a preacher backslide. She crossed her legs and his eyes followed as far as they could see. He was finally next to her and Keisha heart was pounding out of her chest.

"I must compliment you on that outfit," he whispered in her ear.

"This old thing—"

"And here I was thinking you bought that just for me."

"You are not that important."

"Ouch, that hurts."

"I guess I deserve that for shutting you down when you tried to throw yourself at me."

"What a joke. I didn't throw myself at you. I just wanted an interview for my magazine. But your little poodle's bark was much bigger than his bite. Is he going to come running after his master?"

Bling laughed at her sense of humor. She got off the stool because she wanted to go somewhere quiet and talk but she didn't want to ask and get shut down. He was into her so she had to make her move now. She proceeded to the hall without looking back. *I hope he's following me.*

Sure enough he was. "Now you are walking away from me?"

"I just want to go somewhere quiet." She turned to face him. "Let me introduce myself. My name is Keisha and I'm here doing my job." She went into her purse and took out a notepad and a pen to further sell her lies.

"Your job is to pick up guys at the club?"

"I'm here on assignment to interview upcoming artists, like you, who I think have the potential to succeed." She wrote the month, date, and year on the paper.

"And I was thinking you just wanted to get me into your bed."

"You're very attractive. I can give you that but I'm not that easy. Do you mind answering a few questions?"

He put his hand up as if he were at a courthouse swearing in. "I promise to tell the truth and nothing but the truth."

"Why aren't you signed to a label as yet?"

"I have a couple of labels coming at me but I just don't want to sign a contract and then get trapped. There are a lot of deceivers out there."

"There are labels out there that would want to see you succeed."

"There are other talents here tonight; why did you choose me?"

"I know good talent when I see it. I just don't want to see it go to waste. My brother was talented just like you but his career was cut short."

Bling gave a chuckle. "What happened? He lost his voice? Cat got his tongue?"

Keisha's face suddenly turned sad. She closed her notepad and put it back into her purse. She wiped her eyes, making an illusion to seem as if she was crying.

"Did I say something wrong?"

"My brother died a year ago in a car accident."

"I wouldn't make a joke like that if I had known."

"He was all I had. He took care of me when my mother and father turned their backs on me. I miss him a lot."

She put on the waterworks, crying for the dead brother she never had. Poor Bling didn't know that he was face-to-face with an Emmy winner. He fell for it hook, line, and sinker. Bling wrapped his arms around her and gave her a tight hug, but behind his back she wore a big deceiving smile on her face.

"I'm drawn to you because you are so much like him. He was signed to Top Dot Records. They took good care of him. I can honestly say you should sign with them. They are good people."

"I've been approached be so many labels but that name sounds familiar."

"Trust me. He is the best."

"You talk as if you know him personally."

"I do a lot of research on all these labels and Top Dot always comes out on top. Their artists are always first priority. I wouldn't steer you wrong. What would be my gain?"

She modeled a big deceiving smile because she knew she had just sold her lie, a lie that would make her $5,000 richer even if she had to conjure up another lie if he didn't fall for this one.

"Signing with Top Dot would be the best decision you make toward your career."

"I'll keep that in mind, miss career advisor. So you enjoyed my performance that much you had to see it twice?"

"Your performance was great and you aren't too bad to look at."

He took a drink from his glass and emptied it. He wanted to return the compliment but he was afraid that it would send the wrong message. Keisha knew exactly what he was thinking even though he was putting on a front.

"Before this goes any further I have to tell you that I'm happily married."

"I wouldn't say that out loud for your fans to hear. You would definitely have no fans at the end of the night."

"My fans are loyal." He waved to a few fans awaiting his autograph but quickly brought his attention back to Keisha.

"How does your wife feel about all these groupies chasing after you?"

"She knows they're just my fans; and, besides, these groupies as you call them are going to make me rich. So she loves them as much as I do and besides she already got the ring."

"That simply means they can't get a ring, but they can get something else."

"Are we talking about my fans or you?"

"Don't flatter yourself. I'm here doing a job so I have to ask these questions and, besides, I don't mix business with pleasure."

Keisha walked away from him, dropping her made-up business card with her number and home address, knowing he would pick it up. You could tell he didn't want the interview to be over. This time he wanted to be the interviewer because he had questions he wanted to ask her. She knew she had him because his eyes were set on her as she walked away. The first time they met he dismissed her but this time she knew he wanted more. His fans suddenly swarmed him like bees blanketing an intruder trying to take their honey.

He disappeared into the crowd and Keisha exited the club, walking toward her car, when Tina ran after her with a barrage of questions coming at her from all angles. She hadn't spoken to Tina since the fight. *Damn, I didn't know she was at the club tonight.* She didn't let her in on the job she was doing for her uncle. She was always reluctant to fill her in on most ventures that she pursued. Tina was an ego novice who got excited about everything. The men Keisha pursued were white-collar men with families and a lot to lose if their secret was to ever get out. She couldn't afford to let her ruin things for her. Bling was no exception to the rules. This project had to be confidential.

"Are you going to apologize or not?" Tina asked with no confidence.

"Bitch, please. You crossed the line when you keyed my car."

"Keisha, what you did at the restaurant was wrong and you know it."

"He was fair game. He didn't belong to you and, besides, what have you learned from me, Tina?" she asked, still walking to her car.

Tina heels stopped clicking behind her. "You are a heartless bitch."

Keisha turned to face her. "That's right, but a woman without confidence is doomed." She got in her car and drove off, leaving Tina to grow some balls.

Keisha got home and took her clothes off, revealing a matching bra and panties. She lay in her bed, tossing and turning, trying to fall asleep. *I know I made a good impression on Bling. In fact I know he was lusting. I hope he uses my home address because I wrote "home" next to it just in case he needed some more convincing. Am I losing my charm?*

She got out of bed like a zombie, lazily walking to the kitchen. She poured herself a glass of her favorite red wine, gulped it down, then poured another. Her phone was ringing in the bedroom and she ignored it and took another sip of wine and closed her eyes as she swallowed. *What if that's Bling calling?* She opened her eyes wide then put the glass down and ran to the bedroom. She tripped over her shoes, falling flat on her face. She got up, hopping the rest of the way, but still managed to get to the phone on time.

"Hello."

"Do you make a habit of giving strangers your home address?

"Do you make a habit of calling someone this late?"

"Why don't you open the door so I can show you my good and bad habits?"

"I knew you couldn't deprive yourself." She hung up the phone and hurriedly fixed her hair, then walked to the door, exhaling before she opened it.

Bling stood there with both hands placed in his pocket. "You always put your home address on your business card?"

She could read his mind and right then and there she knew he would belong to her for as many hours as he could be with her. She pulled him inside. The passion was there like a burning fire and neither one wanted to put it out. He slammed the door, causing the painting that hung on the wall to fall to the floor. He pushed her against the door and unhooked her bra and filled his mouth with her breast. The warmth of his mouth got her wet instantly. He explored her inner depths with his finger. The combination of his warm tongue and being finger fucked made her juices flow. He released her breasts and brought his finger with her juice to his mouth. Keisha unbuttoned his shirt, then unbuckled his belt, leaving him in his boxers. His body was perfection with no body art in sight. His manhood pointed at her and she was ready for it. He fell on his knees, slowly taking her panties off, revealing her bald pussy. He parted her with his tongue and licked her juice. Keisha held on to his head as his tongue discovered her inner walls.

Remembering she had a roommate she led him to the bedroom. She pushed him against the wall and took his manhood into her hand. His dick was pulsating as well as her clitoris. She opened her mouth and took him in. She did all the tricks she remembered from a Super Head DVD she had seen.

"Oh shit. You the best," he said when her tongue and her hands did a combination. She felt his dick pulsating but she didn't want him to cum so she released him.

She walked over to the bed and lay on her back with her legs wide open, enticing him even more. He wanted to enter but she lengthened her legs to his chest, stopping him. He sucked on her toes and watched her touch herself.

"I see that you are talented in many ways than one."

"Yes, and I'm ready to show you another one of my special talents," Bling bragged.

"Not so fast. You need to promise me that you will sign with Top Dot Records."

"Even during sex you're trying to have me follow in your brother's footsteps. Okay, I promise, only if it will get you to close your mouth and open your legs."

"Tell me that you want me," Keisha teased.

"You know I do."

She playfully called him with her fingers. He placed his hand under her ass and pulled her to the edge of the bed. A fire ignited within her and she wanted to feel his hard dick. "I'm ready for it," Keisha said softly.

She hugged his body and received all of him. He spoke the language of sex and he comprehended every word, sentence, and paragraph. In that moment his wife was nonexistent and Keisha was the star of the show.

Nikki woke up to a mating session. The sound of passion greeted her ear as erotic sounds echoed throughout the house. It couldn't be worse timing because Nikki was just dreaming about Mark hammering her body. She tried blocking out the sound with the pillow over her head but it wasn't helping.

Nikki tossed and turned because she was sexually frustrated. Not to mention that she was getting turned on by Keisha's moans. Nikki couldn't deny herself the pleasure of touching herself so she went into her secret hiding place where she kept her sex toys away from wandering eyes. She took out her vibrator and stripped down to her birthday suit and began pleasuring herself. She adjusted the vibrator speed to high and her clitoris amplified with pleasure. Her moans met Keisha's moans and they were in sync with each other. Nikki bit her lip and closed her eyes.

The thought of Mark opening her door and parting her legs, heightened her ecstasy. She wanted to feel his inflated manhood. Keisha let out a blaring scream because she was conquered by pleasure. The thought brought Nikki to her climax and she exploded. Nikki lay on her back, trying to dismiss the shakiness in her legs and the trembles in her body.

Keisha and Bling lay naked, sound asleep. Her head was on his chest with her arms around him. The hours were slipping by and they slept like babies. His phone rang nonstop but he was out cold so it didn't wake him up. Four hours had elapsed and the alarm went off. He turned his head, looking at the time on the digital clock that was on the nightstand. He couldn't believe his eyes. It was 7:30 a.m. He quickly jumped up with no regard if she woke up. He put on his boxers and hurried to the living room and picked up his clothes off the floor. Keisha wrapped herself in the sheet and followed him. He picked up his clothes piece by piece as he followed the trail to the door.

"How will I explain this to my wife?"

He jumped into his jeans and Keisha picked up his shoes and held them out in her hand. "Just tell her you fell asleep between my legs."

"This was a big mistake."

He opened the door and exited. Keisha closed the door behind him. She felt no remorse, regret, nor hurt because she knew he had to go home to his wife; and, besides, she was just doing a job.

Chapter 11

Nikki's alarm went off for the third time and she hit the snooze button with her head still under the covers. *Just one more minute please. Oh shit! This is my third time pressing the snooze button.* Nikki wrapped herself in the sheets and ran to the bathroom, past Keisha, who was still standing at the front door.

Keisha went into the bathroom after Nikki, who was now in the shower. "So where did you and Mark go last night?"

"Don't even start. I'm late for work."

She got out of the shower and ran to her bedroom without drying her body. But once again Keisha was hot on her trail. "So how is your studying? Isn't your final exam a few days away?"

The outfit Nikki had picked out for work was hanging from her closet door. The white button-down blouse had a big red stain like a bull's-eye on her chest. "What the hell happened to my blouse?"

"Nobody wears your dreary clothes but you, so you should know." Keisha smirked. "So did you fuck him?"

"That's none of your damn business," Nikki yelled from her closet. Nikki settled for a baby blue button down and black-seamed pants.

"Some accessory will bring the dull look to higher heights," Keisha mocked. "I just want to know if it was worth it."

Nikki stopped to address Keisha with one shoe on and the other in her hand. "No, I didn't sleep with Mark. And secondly my sex life, like I said, is none of your damn business."

"As if you really have a sex life." Keisha exited Nikki's bedroom and slammed the door behind her.

It was 9:30 a.m. when Nikki got to her desk and started up her computer. Her boss wasn't in her office so she figured the coast was clear. She had a stack of files piled up on her desk and the only person who could have left them there was her bitch of a boss, Veronica. "That bitch did this on purpose because I was late."

"Call each client and fill in missing information," the sticky note instructed. She scrunched the paper in her hand then tossed it in the trash. One touch of the mouse and her computer screen was up, awaiting her password. Nikki touched each key, wishing it was her boss, Veronica. She wanted poke her eyes out with her index finger. Nikki sat staring at the computer screen and reminisced on her date with Mark. The screen saver came on, indicating that her fingers hadn't stroked a key in minutes.

"Nicolette, is the file I left on you desk ready?" Nikki was still lost in thoughts. "Nicolette!" Veronica spun her chair around.

She came back to reality and saw her boss standing in front of her. "I promise I'll have it to you by lunchtime."

"I would advise you to stay on planet earth because I expect to have all the files on my desk when I get back. All of them."

Nikki despised Veronica because she used her title to her advantage and the only reason why she was promoted was because Nikki had decided to go back to school full time. "She must be crazy. This is more than fifty folders."

Nikki opened the first file and the first sheet was blank, not to mention the other ten sheets in the folder with multiple highlighted areas to fill in. She took the phone off the receiver and poked the telephone number. "May I speak to Mrs. Wilson please?" She took the pen into her hand and prepared to write. "I'm calling from Expedia Mortgage and Loans."

"Special delivery for Nicolette Gray," her noisy co-worker Lashawn loudly announced.

She covered the phone and shooed her away. *How could she know about Mark?* Nikki questioned herself. Lashawn set a bouquet of flowers on her desk.

"Mrs. Wilson, I have to place you on a brief hold." She placed the call on hold and a red light blinked over line one. "What did you just say?"

"Why didn't you tell me that you got married?" she asked with her hand on her hip.

"I'm not married."

"Well this card says differently." Lashawn read the card aloud:

Mrs. Nicolette Gray, these flowers aren't as beautiful as your smile but it's the closest thing in comparison.

"You are holding out on me."

Nikki snatched the card out of her hand. She wasn't ready to answer questions about Mark or to justify him as her man. As a matter of fact she wasn't ready to tell anyone about him. Mark seemed like an okay guy but she couldn't allow herself to let this man into her life. The timing was wrong. She had to focus on studying to pass this test to get into medical school. Passing this test would validate her life and she wasn't going to let Mark distract her from achieving her goal.

"Nicolette. That call has been on hold for five minutes." Lashawn scattered to her cubicle when Veronica approached Nikki's desk.

"Why don't you make your phone calls your damn self? It's your job to gather information not mine." She took her pocketbook and the bouquet of flowers.

Veronica stepped aside and let her pass. "You will get a write up for this!" Veronica shouted at Nikki as she exited the office.

Let someone else do your file, bitch. She strolled down the street and bolted into a coffee shop and got her regular French vanilla. There was an elderly lady sitting by the window. Nikki walked over to her and handed her the bouquet. She turned to walk away but the women got her attention.

"Do you think if you gave it away you can get rid of your feelings?"

"Excuse me?"

"These flowers may not mean much to him but I can tell that they are speaking to your heart."

"You couldn't be further from the truth."

"Come. Sit." The lady patted the seat next to her. "Let this old woman tell you a thing or two about love."

Nikki reluctantly sat next to the old lady. But she was still interested in what the woman had to say. "Before you continue to go on and on about love, I have to tell you that I'm not in love with anyone but my books."

"Yes, I know, my child. You want to make your mother proud. And she is."

"How do you know about that? Did Keisha put you up to this?" She jumped to her feet, furious.

"I must say she is smiling down from above," the old lady continued despite Nikki's outburst.

"Who are you? Are you a psychic or a mind reader?"

"My child, you must be careful of wolves in sheep's clothes," she went on to say, disregarding Nikki's question.

Nikki felt uncomfortable. She grabbed her purse and bolted to the door.

"A lingering lie will fester, but the truth will also cause a wound. Some people are the devil in disguise!" The old lady spoke her last words as Nikki hurried to the door.

Was she talking about someone in my life or someone I've yet to meet?

Chapter 12

"You better get the job done! You know what the plan is so you better stick to it, and remember you have more to lose than I do!"

Keisha ended her conversation and opened the door to her uncle's office. Patrick puffed on a cigar, sitting in his black leather chair with his feet up on his desk. He formed his mouth in the shape of a circle so the smoke would come out looking like halos as it went up over his head. His office was simply decorated. Pictures of Bob Marley hung on each wall. On his desk sat a phone with several magazine scattered on top. There was a wine rack in plain sight and a refrigerator sat in a corner in the back of his office.

"Ummh-ummh." Keisha stood at his office door and cleared her throat.

He spun around in his chair, facing her direction. She walked inside and he stood up and greeted her with a hug. Patrick was very tall, about six feet four inches. He wasn't very handsome but he had attractive features. His high cheekbones and luscious lips weren't enough to overlook his bulging eyeballs. He was dressed in blue jeans and a black blazer with a white shirt inside to match his white sneakers. Patrick looked at his watch, viewing the time. "What brought you here?"

"I was hoping to collect my money."

"I guess that you are under the assumption that the guys had already signed on the dotted lines."

She sat at the opposite end of the table, placing her large pocketbook filled with everything you could imagine at her feet. "So they didn't?"

Patrick poured himself a shot of Hennessy from a bottle that was situated at arm's length on the desk. "Well, Hype signed but Bling didn't show."

"All I had to do was make a few promises to Hype. He even asked me to marry him in our first conversation. His age does show in his conversation. He was a horny puppy. He was such a bore. "

"Maybe it does take more than a pretty face to reel Bling in."

Her ego was shattered. Her bright eyes now became dim. He had promised her that he would. She replayed the words he said over and over in her head to see if she had missed any inclination that she had been misled. *Did he use me for his satisfaction the way I was using him?*

"He will show."

Patrick took the shot to his head and rubbed his chest after he swallowed. She filled her uncle in on the details on how the night went, sparing the details of how the night ended; but when she told him about her Oscar-winning performance about her dead brother he chuckled and puffed on his cigar. The simultaneous beeps from his phone told him his receptionist was calling and he put it on speaker.

"Bling is here to see you, Mr. Burkett."

"Send him in."

Keisha stood on her feet in a panic. "He can't see me here."

He indicated for her to hide in the closet. She picked up her pocketbook and ran to the closet, nesting there with the door ajar. Patrick took his seat in his big black leather recliner chair, puffing on his cigar, acting nonchalant. Bling entered his office but Patrick didn't get up to greet him. He sat rocking in his chair.

"Have a seat."

Bling sat like an obedient schoolboy because even though he had the upper hand, Patrick was still the big man in charge.

"I don't accept an unscheduled meeting but I'm interested to know what brought you here."

"Word on the street is that you the big man."

"I'm just a man with a plan."

Bling expressed his interest in signing with Top Dot Records. Keisha's smile widened from ear to ear. She hadn't gotten her money as yet but she had already spent it. Her palm itched as she pictured her uncle placing the $5,000 cash in her hand. She was going to pamper herself because it was well deserved. She listened attentively as Patrick highlighted the accomplishments of his company and the success rate of his artists. He went on and on about how he would launch Bling's career. Keisha drifted off into sleep. The signing took longer than she had anticipated. She knew nothing about the music business, the same way she was naïve to the reality of life.

Patrick knocked on the closet door and Keisha held her head up with her eyes open wide. "The coast is clear!" She ran out of the closet like a frolicking pony. Patrick removed a picture from the wall, exposing a safe. He gave her $5,000 cash.

"Thanks, Uncle, we should do business again."

"Well, it's funny that you should say that because I do have another job for you."

"I will do it. But this time my rate is double."

Keisha's phone made a peep indicating that she had a text message. She located the phone and saw that it was Martin. She retrieved the message.

I would love to take you out to dinner tonight. I miss your beautiful smile. Meet me at our favorite restaurant around 8:00 p.m. You know our secret hideaway.

Keisha's finger massaged the keys as she replied,

I accept.

Besides, tonight was her only free time because she was
going to have her hands full for a while.

"Well, Uncle, we have a deal so text me his information
so I can get the ball rolling. You are going to have to make
me a business partner soon."

"Yes, but a silent one."

They both laughed and Keisha left the office. After
running some errands she got home a little after six. She
entered the house to the sound of a whistling kettle and
she went to the kitchen. Nikki was sitting at the table with
her head in a book, sleeping. *This bitch is trying to burn
my damn house down.* She turned the knob to off. She
didn't bother to wake Nikki.

She went straight to her bedroom. Mr. Money wanted
to meet up at eight and that didn't leave her with much
time. She knew exactly what she would wear on the date.
It was a chic little black dress with the back cut out. She
took a quick shower, which left her with not enough time
to get dressed.

When she got to the restaurant Mr. Money was already
there waiting for her outside. She was late as usual and he
was a little irritable because time was of the essence with
him. She walked up to him with a radiant smile. He had
no choice but to replace his frown because her beauty was
tantalizing. Mr. Money extended his arm and greeted her
with a tight hug.

"You look exquisite as usual."

"You bought me this dress, don't you remember?"

They held hands as they strolled into the restaurant. They
were escorted to their table and he pulled out her chair,
unlike David. The burning candle situated in the center of
the table added a romantic accent to the atmosphere. Mr.
Money complimented her look and took her hand, greeting

it with a kiss. He was a quite the gentleman but also very arrogant. Mr. Money was an entrepreneur, the CEO of a magazine company, and he was also a radio personality. He was a little cocky because he was his own boss.

His phone rang and he excused himself, leaving Keisha at the table. Keisha occupied herself by scrolling through the menu, not quite sure if she wanted seafood or steak. A sudden outburst of excitement made her drop the menu and brought her attention to the table straight ahead but slightly to her left. A woman's eyes widened as if she had seen the biggest diamond ever found in Africa. The woman was now reading a document and every word out her mouth was "Oh my God." The man's back was turned to Keisha so she couldn't see his face.

It can't be divorce papers because she is way too happy. Keisha brought her attention back to the menu. *Filet mignon it is.* She closed the menu and witnessed the couple sharing a hug. Keisha tried to get a better look at the man's face but Mr. Money blocked her view as the man turned to get the waiter's attention.

"It seems as if you're more interested in what's going on over there."

What the hell? I can't catch a break. This is probably good gossip. Could be the husband of someone I know. Maybe I should just be outright nosy and go to the lady's room; it's in that direction.

"Okay, point taken. Now you have my undivided attention."

"I just wanted to let you know that I'm doing a column in my magazine about curvaceous women and I want you to be one of the featured women."

From sideways his facial feature looks familiar to her. She could see a waiter walking to their table with a bottle of champagne.

Keisha didn't hear a single word that Mr. Money had said. She wanted so badly to solve this mystery. But once again her view was blocked as the waiter approached Keisha's table.

"Are you ready to order?"

"What are you in the mood for?" her date irritably asked.

"Go ahead and order for me."

Keisha leaned her head sideways, still in investigative mood. Mr. Money already knew what he wanted so he ordered the same for her. He turned his head, following Keisha's stare to see what was distracting her. The man turned his head, acknowledging the waiter, and Keisha gasped.

"Bling!" she blurted out. "It can't be," she said out loud, and Mr. Money looked at her questioningly.

"Is there a problem?"

She was incognizant of Mr. Money's question.

"Do you know him?"

The waiter came back with the tequila just in time to intercept Mr. Money's question. She had no idea what he had ordered but she drank it so fast you would have thought she was in the Sahara Desert dying of thirst.

"So tell me about the work you are doing on your house." She quickly changed the subject. She didn't want to explain or answer any questions about Bling.

"I'm just going green that's all."

Keisha was making small talk but she was no longer interested in him or what he had to say. The man who was in her bed last night was a few feet away from her with his wife. She now knew what she was so exited about. *He should be celebrating with me. I'm the reason why he signed the damn contract.* She was pleasantly surprised when the waiter returned with the main course it was filet mignon and sweet potato. It was just what her palate needed because the sight of Bling's wife left a bitter taste in her mouth.

Bling's wife was the quintessential true beauty. You could tell she was in love with her husband. She gazed at him and the happiness from her heart reflected in her eyes. Keisha was still in the middle of her meal but Keisha wanted out. Seeing Bling with his wife made her nauseous.

"I don't feel too good."

"Is there any thing I can do?" Mr. Money inquired.

"I just need to get some rest, that's all." She wiped her mouth with the napkin and stood to her feet. Mr. Money also rose to his feet. "Please finish your meal. I'm a big girl. I can take care of myself." He kissed her cheek and he watched her walked away.

The drive home was confusing to Keisha. She wasn't sure what she was upset about. Yes, she had spent the night with Bling, but it was just for business. She had no reason to be upset or even jealous. All she knew was that her blood was boiling. Deep down inside she felt insecure. Keisha was threatened by Bling's wife's beauty. For the first time in a long time she wanted to be loved. She wanted to be touched by him. His kisses had sent shivers up her spine. His touches were magical. She had an icebox where her heart used to be but he had managed to melt it. Seeing how her father had treated her mother, not to mention that her first love had broken her heart many years ago, made her vow never to let a man close to her heart again. Seeing Bling sharing laughs and celebrating with his wife made her jealous. Even though Bling had cheated on his wife she was willing to make an exception to the rule. Even though it was a one-night stand her body wanted him and she wasn't going to deprive herself. She wanted him even if she was going to share him with his wife.

She finally made it home and pulled into the driveway. The outside light came on, giving her a clear view. She stepped out of her car with her shoes in her hand because even though her shoes cost more than an average person's weekly paycheck they still hurt her feet. There was an envelope pasted to her door, addressed to her from her father. She wanted to rip it to shreds and watch the torn pieces fall to the ground like snow. She reluctantly opened the envelope.

I'm disappointed in the woman you have become. But you are still my daughter. I've made mistakes but I also learned from them. I'm asking for your forgiveness because I am a better man.

Not wanting to read her father's apology she ripped the note to shreds. She noticed Johnny's car parked on the opposite side of the street. He was watching her every move. She noticed his car following her today but she knew Johnny was harmless. She opened the door, stripping off her clothes as she entered the house. She remained in her pink lace bra and panties as she strolled to the kitchen to pour a glass of her favorite red wine. Drinking red wine was a ritual that she preformed to calm her nerves. She gulped one glass and poured another for the walk back to the bedroom.

She couldn't get the image of Bling and his wife out of her head. *Why is it upsetting me? I can't possibly have feelings for Bling. I did my job and that's it.* She took a sip of wine, trying to rid her mind of the thoughts. On her way back from the kitchen she almost has a heart attack when she saw Bling standing at the door. "How did you get in?"

"Here I was thinking that you left the door open for me."

"And why would I do that?"

"Well you need to get that lock fixed. It seems to be tampered with."

"What are you doing here?"

Bling took the contract out of his pocket and gave it to her. She viewed the document and passed it back to him. "Did I have something to do with your hasty decision?"

"Yes, you did. And that's the reason why I'm here."

"So you can thank me in person?"

"That too but—"

"If you are here to take me on tour with you I would have to turn down your offer because you are married and I wouldn't want to break up a happy home."

"That's the other reason why I'm here. I'm a married man and I love my wife. We can't see each other again."

"It was supposed to be a one-night stand. One night only, remember? Go home, Bling. Go back to your boring sex life with your so-called wife. Your secret is safe with me."

Keisha's ego was hurt but she wasn't going to let it show. She was good at what she did and she knew it. She also knew that his wife wasn't even close in comparison.

"I shouldn't have gotten caught up in this nonsense with you in the first place. I can't mess up a good thing with my wife for you."

Bling's words were cutting her like a knife whether he knew it or not, and she lashed back at him with venom in her tongue like a snake. "Why are you really here? We didn't have to see each other again. To my knowledge it was supposed to be a one-night stand but here you are professing your love for your wife. Tell me something, Bling. Are you confessing your love for your wife to hide the real reason why you're here?"

Bling turned to walk away but she grabbed his arm, pulling him closer to her and seductively sliding her finger down his face, testing his sincerity. "You want more of me, admit it."

"I love my wife."

"Okay, you are free to go. Walk out the door and we never have to see each other again."

Bling walked to the door and fumbled with the lock. She removed his hand and opened the door, making it clear that he was free to go. He slammed the door and braced her against it.

"So you like to play rough. I like it rough," she said naughtily.

"I love my wife," he said as if he was trying to convince himself.

"I'm not asking you to love me."

He kissed her lips and it ignited a burning fire within them that neither had the energy to put out. She proceeded to unbutton his shirt while he continued to enjoy her soft lips.

"I can't do this."

"You aren't doing anything. I am."

He couldn't resist. He gave into her and kissed her with a passion as if he was trying to add gasoline to an already-burning fire. Once again the love for his wife was not enough to resist Keisha. She also knew her craft and didn't hesitate to use it to her advantage. They enjoyed each other right there on the carpeted floor. She didn't have a second thought that Nikki might exit her room and see them. His moves were in sync with hers. His body spoke and she responded to every stroke as if they were old acquaintances who understood each other's rhythm. He was gentle with her body as if she was someone he wanted to cherish. Keisha held him tight and every muscle in his body tightened and extended and she felt him even more. He raised his head and acknowledged her breast, caressing her nipple with his warm tongue.

His playful tongue transferred a sensation throughout her body, which caused her to detonate like a bomb. He kissed her lips. She bit on to his because he was close to his climax and his strokes intensified. He roared like a lion from pleasure and the pain of her teeth piercing his lip. She wanted all of him and he gave it to her. They held each other and took deep breaths because that ride took them on a high that only oxygen could make subside.

Chapter 13

"Can I have French vanilla with two croissants please?" Nikki turned her body, hoping to see the old lady again. But there was no sign of her. Nikki had gone to the diner deliberately to see the old lady.

"Excuse me!" She got the waitress's attention. "I was here a few days ago and . . . I know this is going to sound strange but there was an old lady sitting at the window. Did you happen to see her this morning?"

The waitress shook her head. "No, I haven't." She placed the coffee on the counter with the croissant. "That will be $3.75."

Nikki handed her a five dollar bill and extended her arm for her change. Nikki took a seat by the window purposely so she could get an outside view. She had an urgency to see the old lady again because her word lingered on her mind.

She wrapped her fingers around the warm cup and inhaled the aroma of the French vanilla. She took a sip, awaking her taste buds. The warm liquid slowly went down the back of her throat. "Mmh." She took a bite from the soft, buttery croissant and quickly took another. She finished both croissants in record time. Her appetite was open this morning. She wanted another but she had to control herself.

She sipped her coffee and a loud burp came from the pit of her belly, escaping through her lips. Nikki embarrassingly placed her hand over her mouth and turned her head, looking to see if anyone was looking at her. "I guess that's my queue to leave."

She approached the door and a man entering at the same time held it open for her. She gave him a smile and kept it moving. She paced her steps to a slow crawl and sipped her coffee. She approached a bus stop; anxiety took over her body. She thought that the old lady could be at the bus stop and she sped up her step. For some strange reason she thought the old lady held the answer to her future. She had no reason to stop when she made it to the bus stop, so she scanned the box-shaped waiting area with her eyes and beheld a gray-haired lady wearing a black hat searching in her pocketbook.

"I've been looking for you!" Nikki quick stepped to the lady, grabbing her shoulder. "I need to know my future."

Everyone looked at Nikki as if she was crazy. The old lady looked up at her and waved her off, spilling the coffee.

"I'm so sorry," Nikki apologetically said.

"I'm not a damn fortune teller. Get away from me!"

Nikki backed away, "I thought you were someone else." Nikki hurried off. *What am I doing? Get yourself together, girl. Are you going crazy?*

Nikki wanted to know if she had a future with Mark. Her body was calling for him, her heart already accepted him, her mind was captivated by him, and her soul wanted to spend forever with him. "After all, my relationship with Mark is blooming." Everything was perfect. "God has sent me Mr. Right. The old lady at the diner didn't know what she was talking about. Why do I doubt my relationship when everything is perfect? The only vindictive person in my life is Keisha, and I already know she is a wolf. What does she has up her sleeves?"

Nikki waited for the elevator to descend. She was early for work but dreaded going into that office; besides, she knew the files were still on her desk, waiting for her. Finally the elevator door opened and she got in and pressed the button for the third floor. It was a straight ride up. No one got on or off.

"Good morning," she greeted the receptionist.

She heard, "Nicolette! In my office please," before she made it to her desk. Mr. Troop summoned her. She wished she could click her heels three times and disappear.

"Good morning, Mr. Troop."

"Close the door behind you," he ordered with his eyes still on his computer screen.

This can't be good. I know the bitch Veronica had to say something.

"Veronica left a complaint on my desk about you not doing your job." He took his glasses off and crossed his arms on his chest.

Nikki sat up in her chair. "The truth of the matter is Veronica wants me to do more than my job. The problem is that I refrained from doing her job."

"Nikki, you are an asset to this company but you can easily be replaced. I am the CEO of this company. So if you and Veronica can't get it together I will have to let one of you go."

"Yes, sir."

"You are dismissed." He put his glasses back on his big face. Nikki got up and turned the knob to open the door but there was a knock at the door. "Come in!" Mr. Troop instructed.

Nikki opened the door and saw Veronica. She pushed her a few steps backward and quickly closed the door so Mr. Troop wouldn't see the confrontation. "So because you are sucking off the boss's pipes you run shit around here?"

"Is that what you just did in there? How was it?" she asked with a smile on her face.

"You are sick and disgusting. I will not be sharing anything, not even a drink of water if you are dying."

"So because I decide to secure my job so I can keep food on my table you are degrading me? Child, please. A woman got to do what a woman got to do."

"Your ass will be out of here as soon as he gets tired of you."

"Well, it's about that time. You are welcome to join and from the looks of things you might want to secure your job." She walked past Nikki, bumping into her shoulder.

Nikki wanted to scratch her eyes out but she held her composure.

Nikki wanted to use one of her personal days but she couldn't just leave now. Nikki sat at her desk and went through as many files as she could until her workday ended. There was a dock in close proximity of her workplace so she took a stroll. Being around water always seemed to cure her stress. Being in that office with bonus-hungry bitches and people trying to close on a sale by deadline, not to mention the backstabbers, would make anybody stress.

Amid a few trees a lighthouse stood guard, proudly sporting its red and white stripes. There was a boat in the distance and she thought how beautiful it would be if it were her on that boat making love to Mark for the first time, gliding on water. Nikki reached for her cell phone and dialed Mark.

He answered on the first ring. "Are you calling to tell me you miss me?"

"Don't hold your breath. Are you interested in catching an early movie?"

"Aren't you at work?"

"No. But can you pick me up at the boardwalk on Marina Drive by my job."

"Okay. I'll be there in a few."

Nikki took her attention back to the gliding boat. She imagined how beautiful making love to Mark would be for the first time. But Keisha kept popping up in her thoughts. *Why was she so interested in whether I had made love to Mark?* Keisha was a conniving bitch but to ruin her relationship with Mark was unthinkable.

Mark got to the dock in less than five minutes. Nikki didn't even notice him admiring her. Her high cheekbones and thick lips defined her beauty.

Mark hugged her around her waist. "I'll give you a penny for your thoughts."

"Are you trying to kill me?"

"Why would I? How would I live without you?" He spun her around and kissed her softly.

Nikki could feel all her muscles loosen. Her body wanted him but she wasn't ready to give in. She wanted him to prove himself before she gave up her goodies. "Are you ready to go?"

"How about if we do movies at your place instead so we can get cozy?" He still held on to her.

"That's not a good idea because with you being there I won't have time to catch up on my studies." Lately she had been slacking on studying. She was so caught up in this romance with Mark and that's one thing she had vowed to herself that she would never do. Mark came on strong. He had turned her no into yes. He swept her off her feet with his bold talks of plans, ideas, and aspirations for his future. He had a vision for life and that's exactly what she liked in a man.

"Come on. Those books can't love you like I can."

"On second thought, how about if we go to the movies another time? I'm just going to get some ice cream to go."

"I'll take Nikki with a cherry on top." He kissed her lips. "You are my dark chocolate."

He picked her up and carried her to his blue two-door sports car. He brought her to the driver side and handed her the key. She wrinkled her brow, shaking her head no. This car was a fast car; plus, the idea of learning to drive stick shift never crossed her mind.

"Today I put my life in your hands." He sat in the passenger seat and put his feet up on the dashboard while Nikki stood still, staring down at the key in her hand.

"This car can't drive itself," Mark taunted. He reclined his seat and got comfortable. Nikki tried desperately to talk Mark out of letting her drive his car but to no avail. He gave her a quick crash course of how the gas pedal and clutch worked like a team. Her first attempt ended up in a sudden jolt; so did the second, third, and fourth.

"Come on, Miss College Student, this isn't rocket science."

His statement rubbed her the wrong way and it got her blood boiling. She had no interest in learning before but now she was going to prove to him it really wasn't rocket science. Nikki adjusted her seat and also her rearview mirror. She looked him in his face, sizing him up.

"If you can do it, a strong woman like me can do it even better. I just have to put pedal to the metal right?"

She turned the key in the ignition and before he could say a word she took off with high speed. She screamed out in excitement and laughter because she surprised herself. He sat upright in his seat, begging her to slow down. She turned the music up so she wouldn't have to hear his plea. She gave him the ride of his life, one he would never forget. She pulled up at the ice cream shop and tossed the key into his lap. Mark sat there wide-eyed, trying to comprehend what just happened.

"I'll order to go. Stay seated just in case you pissed on yourself." Mark checked himself to make sure he didn't piss his pants because it sure felt like he did. Nikki exited the car, laughing. Without hesitation Mark jumped into the driver seat as if he were sitting on hot bricks. Mark was convinced that Nikki knew how to drive stick all along and she couldn't tell him otherwise.

Nikki had a taste for rum raisin ice cream but her mouth watered for a taste of the other flavors. It was her turn to order but she was still undecided. She finally settled for a scoop of pistachio and two scoops of rum raisin. When she went outside Mark was on his phone but he ended his call when he saw her approaching. "I thought I would get to drive home."

"Never again," Mark replied as he drove off.

"Never say never," she added with a smile.

They pulled up to the house and Nikki got out of the car and blew him a kiss, disregarding his plea to come inside. She got to the door and realized that she had left the ice cream in the car. She turned her head only to see Mark stretching the bag out the window.

"You forgot something," Mark sang.

She headed back to the car and took the bag out his hand. Mark made the impression of a sad puppy dog face and she gave him a kiss on his cheek, turning his frown into a bright smile. She smiled at his boyish behavior as she walked back to the door. She barely got inside the house when the phone started ringing. Without hesitation she answered her phone.

"I miss you," Mark's voice said on the other end.

"I'm not going let you change my mind. I have to study. Bye, Mark, I'll talk to you later."

She hung up the phone and took her shoes off. She wasn't sure what to think about Mark. She had fallen for him and wanted to give herself to him but she wanted it to be special.

"All I want to do right now is enjoy my ice cream with the company of my books." Nikki set the ice cream on the table and headed to the living room, where she last sat reading her book. She saw her notebook but the textbook was missing. She was puzzled but optimistically walked to her bedroom, searching through the stack of books she had piled up on the floor; but the book was nowhere in sight.

"Where the hell could it be?"

She tried to retrace her every move. The last place she remembered leaving the book was right on the table, which now only accommodated the centerpiece and her notebook. She tossed the cushions from a chair. She emptied her pocketbook. She hastily walked to the kitchen, opening the cabinets and drawers, hoping that maybe she was sleepwalking and placed it there. Nikki couldn't afford to buy another textbook, and, besides, she wasn't getting paid for another two weeks and she needed it right now.

"Where is my damn book?"

Nikki searched high and low trying to locate her book, but to no avail. "Could I have possible left it at the library?" She opted for a glass of water then remembered that she hadn't eaten her ice cream. It was the perfect time to enjoy her ice cream because she was sweating from the turmoil of trying to find her textbook.

She sat at the table, putting her hair up into a bun. Her skin was moist with sweat, as if she was smothered in baby oil. She opened the carton and the ice cream was melting rapidly. The AC was off and it was midsummer. She dipped the spoon and came up, aiming for her mouth. She closed her eyes and reached for the spoon with her tongue. Nikki lets out a pleased sound as the ice cream awakened her taste buds. She tightened her lips and sucked the spoon dry and went for another dip. The process was repeated until the carton was empty. She felt guilty afterward for subjecting her body to all those calories.

Nikki approached the garbage can and stepped on the lever and the lid flew open. She dropped the ice cream container but something in the trash can caught her eye. She quickly lowered her arm and came up with her textbook. "What the hell? How did my book get in there?"

She couldn't put one and one together to come up with two. She had no explanation other than she might have dropped it in by accident. By this time her mind was off studying. The ice cream was like an aphrodisiac and it was transferring signals to her brain, and they had nothing to do with studying. She had been denying herself a man for so long and her body was in rebellious mode. She was horny and she needed the touch of a man. *Maybe a cold shower will help.*

She ran to the bathroom and stripped off her clothes, but she saw her reflection in mirror and her naked body spoke a silent language. Her seductive eyes pled with her. Her thick lips begged to be kiss. Her firm breasts longed for the caress of a man's hand. She turned the faucet on and stepped inside the tub. She was trying to control the urges but it was in vain. She imagined as the warm water ran down her body and it brought her to think of that day when she saw Mark at the park with sweat running down his chiseled body. The hard metal faucet had her imaging Mark standing naked in front of her with his manhood standing firm.

Taking a shower wasn't helping at all. She got out of the shower, trying to run away from her wild imagination. She covered herself with a towel and hastily walked to her bedroom. She took a deep breath and dialed Mark's number. He picked up on the first ring.

"I need you," Nikki said without hesitation.

That was all Mark needed to hear. He was there in no time, as if he had been lurking around the corner awaiting her phone call. She opened the door and escorted him inside her bedroom, closing the door behind him. She dropped her towel and his mouth widened.

"Is this what you want?"

He nodded his head like a bobble-head doll. She used her finger and pushed his chin up to close his mouth. She sat on the edge of the bed and parted her legs. He swallowed hard. He tried to speak but he was still at a loss for words.

"Take your shirt off," she instructed and he complied. "If you want it, come and get it."

Mark was in shock. He didn't know who this woman was. This wasn't the Nikki he knew. This woman wanted sex. Studying was far from her mind. He grabbed her face and passionately kissed her. She unbuckled his belt and his pants fell to the ground. She stood up and pressed her body against his naked chest and felt his heartbeat. She wanted to be one with him so she hugged him tight. She felt his hands grip her ass and she panicked.

"What am I doing?" She backed away from him.

"Please don't stop," Mark begged.

"I can't do this." She tried to cover herself. "This was a mistake. You have to leave! I have to study."

"When are you going to stop hiding behind your damn books?"

"Is that how you see it? My books were here before you and will be here after you."

"I didn't mean to offend you," Mark said apologetically. "But I know you are hiding behind your books to protect your heart." Mark held her in his arms. "You don't need to be scared. I'm here to love you. Look at me." Mark spun her around. "I love you. I love you, Nicolette."

Tears ran from her eyes. He kissed her lips and she didn't refuse him. He lifted her off her feet and placed her on the bed. He wiped the tears from her face and kissed her lips again. He slithered his tongue down her body and he kissed every part of her. She released her fears and spread her legs open. He parted her bush forest and found her pot of gold.

"Open your eyes. Look at me. I'm here for you."

Nikki looked at the man who was giving her sensations she hadn't felt in years. Her legs trembled.

"Let it out, baby. Don't hold back." Mark spread her legs with his hand and kept his head in her center, He knew she was ready for him and he entered her. Nikki clung on to him when she felt his manhood inside her. He filled her up with little room to maneuver. He was gentle with her. They found their grove. He made love to her mind, body, and soul.

Things were too calm around the house lately. A storm was brewing somewhere and trust me it was about to hit with mighty force. Keisha pushed Nikki's door open like a raging bull. Nikki and Mark franticly hid their naked bodies under the sheet as Keisha's mouth spit fire like an angry dragon.

"You fucking bitch!" Keisha yelled.

"Get out!" Nikki screamed

"This isn't a whorehouse!" Keisha hollered

"Get out!"

"This is not a hotel so I will suggest you take your fuck fest somewhere else. And secondly the rent is due so I hope you he's paying you."

Keisha exited the room, leaving the door open behind her. Nikki was confused. She didn't know what to make of what just happened. She wasn't sleeping with Keisha's man. Feeling humiliated and belittled she hid her face under the sheet. Mark wanted to stay with her but she told him to leave. She wrapped herself in the sheet and hurried to Keisha's bedroom, almost tripping as she walked. She pushed the door and entered but Keisha wasn't there. She raced to the bathroom but still couldn't find her. Her last stop was the kitchen, which was to be expected because she never resisted a glass of red wine.

"Look what the cat dragged in." Keisha laughed and raised her glass to Nikki. "Were you that boring in bed that he didn't stay for seconds?" Keisha teased, knowing damn well what she had done.

"You shut your damn mouth because that is the last time you will ever disrespect me like that again."

"I'm so scared." Keisha rolled her eyes. "I should have known that you were really a bitch!" Nikki stepped to her and Keisha also took a step forward. "You need to take a couple of steps back and realize whose house you're in."

"Trust me, I know where I am."

"Do you really? Because I don't understand why you would be here acting like you're in charge."

"Give me one good reason why I shouldn't tear you apart right now."

"You have ten seconds to get the hell out my face before I throw you out my house."

"You are a jealous, pathetic bitch!"

"Now you have five seconds."

"You can't stand to see someone happier than you?"

"Oh, please." Keisha walked away from her. "You can't even see the truth when it's right in front of you."

"You are so right. I see it clearly now. You are nothing but a jealous bitch!"

"You are an unappreciative bitch! After all I did for you. I'm looking out for you and this is how you repay me."

"Are you really looking out for me? Is that what you call it? You barged into my room and insulted me."

"You insult yourself by sleeping with a man you don't even know. He wanted one thing and you just gave it up."

"That's none of you damn business."

"Can't say I never warned you."

"He chose classy over trashy and you just can't stand it." Nikki got the last word.

Nikki walked away, leaving Keisha to drown her jealousy in her red wine. Keisha had a sinister look on her face as she watched her walk away. She rose her glass to her lips and finished her wine. It didn't matter much to Keisha if Nikki never spoke to her again; besides, her life was too busy for her to think about anybody's feelings other than her own.

Chapter 14

"You need to pack a suitcase. I'm taking you with me to Jamaica for the weekend. Be ready in an hour."

"Bling, it's short notice." She tried to disguise her excitement. Keisha was jumping up and down in her bed. Unbeknownst to Bling, she was ready to go.

"It's only going to be for the weekend. I have to perform at ATI in Negril. Pack light."

"Bling, I can't. I have to—"

"What can be more important than going away with me?" Bling cut her off in midsentence.

Actually nothing was more important to Keisha because Keisha was already taking clothes out of her closet. "I just have to cancel a few appointments."

"I'll be there in an hour." Click. He hung up before she could say another word.

Keisha took out her Louis Vuitton duffle bag from under the bed. She didn't have to second-guess what she was going to pack because she had outfits for all occasions. The duffle bag was stuffed with clothes and shoes within minutes.

She remembered she had forgotten to pack the most important items of all and she hurried to her lingerie drawer. She had lingerie of all colors and style. "This is the winner for tonight." She held up a red teddy with matching crotch-less panties. "You don't even have to take these off, baby." She tossed in a bunch of edible panties. Keisha picked out some more lingerie and stuffed it into the bag that was obviously full to capacity. Keisha was packing in excitement, knowing the erotic nights and days that awaited her.

Keisha put her legs in a jean miniskirt and danced and wiggled herself into it. "Damn! I have to shave my legs." Keisha ran to the bathroom and plastered her legs with Nair to remove the hair. She washed her hands and did her makeup while she waited for the Nair to do its job. She did her makeup light but the pink eye shadow was heavy over her eyes. The pink lip gloss made her full lips plump. She combed through her wrap and the sixteen-inch weave resting on her back. Nicki Minaj had nothing on her.

The Nair was starting to irritate her legs. It was burning and she knew it was time to wash the chemical off. She took a washcloth and wiped her legs. The hair came off, leaving her legs smooth to the touch. Keisha still had ten minutes to finish getting dressed. She applied Victoria's Secret lotion to her legs and they were as smooth as a baby's butt.

Keisha went to put her blouse on but knew instantly it was a bad idea to do her makeup first. "Why didn't I put my blouse on before I did my makeup?" She had intended to put on a white blouse but it would definitely get soiled if she tried putting it over her head. "I guess I have to enter from bottom up." Keisha put her legs in and tried to get it over her skirt, and a few threads popped along the way but they weren't visible to the eye. The white Guess off-the-shoulder blouse hugged her breasts and her waist, giving her an hourglass shape. Her pink Guess six-inch high-heel pumps went with her pink clutch purse.

She pulled her Louis Vuitton duffle to the door. Beep. Beep. A loud horn sounded outside. Before she could open the door the horn was going off again. She opened the door and Bling's driver got out of the car. "I'm coming! I'm coming!" The man ran up the steps to get her bag.

"You know it's bumper-to-bumper traffic on I-95 to JFK Airport this time of day. And make sure you have your passport," Bling shouted from the back seat of the black Lexus.

"Oh shit." She hurried to her bedroom. She knew exactly where to find it. She pulled out the nightstand drawer and took it out. She exited the house and Bling whistled. She got in the back seat with Bling and her jean miniskirt went up a few more inches when she sat. Bling glided his hand up her skirt.

"Not here." She removed his hand.

"Don't mind me. I hear no evil, see no evil," the driver assured them.

Bling laughed at his friend's humor. "I'm not giving you a show, you pervert."

Keisha rolled her eyes at him. Her phone started to ring in her pocketbook and she answered it. "Listen, I can't talk to you right now. I'm going away for the weekend but that doesn't mean it's time off for you. You know what to do so do it. The plan is still in motion so stick to it." She ended her conversation.

"What's that about?"

"Work as usual." Keisha dismissed his inquiry.

The hour-and-a-half ride took almost three thanks to roadwork.

"Last call for flight number 376." The announcement echoed over the speaker at JFK. They rushed to check in, just barely making the flight.

The seat belt sign came on and they buckled up. "I'm scared of heights. I'm scared of flying. Why did I let you talk me into this?" Keisha was using her hands to cover her face. Being excited about going away with Bling made her forget about her fear of flying but now her fears were back. The last time she went to Florida for her birthday with Mr. Money turbulence had made her fear heighten and she hadn't flown since then.

"Relax, I'm right here. What could go wrong?"

The plane lifted up in the air and Keisha was hyperventilating. "Oh, my God! Oh, my God." Bling was laughing hysterically. "It's not funny."

He put his arms around her, bringing her closer to him. "Just breathe."

Keisha actually felt safe in his arms. She managed to calm herself down and relax.

It wasn't long before Bling had fallen asleep with his arms still cuddling Keisha. Keisha watched his nostrils flare up and down as he inhaled and exhaled. She glided her finger across his bushy eyebrow, smiling at the thought of how handsome their baby would be. She laid her head back and closed her eyes and exhaled.

The resort in Negril, Jamaica was beautiful. Their hotel was overlooking the beach. Keisha viewed the ocean from the balcony. She wanted to go dip her body in the water the minute she arrived. She was away from Nikki and Tina and she couldn't be happier. She was stress free whenever she was with Bling. Keisha was the happiest woman on earth, especially knowing he was with her and not his wife. "Babe, let's go swimming. The water is so beautiful."

"I have to take a rain check. The promoter is picking me up in five minutes. I have to go to the radio station and then I have to meet and greet the fans. But I promise I'll go when I get back."

Bling took his shirt off and his bare chest was like dark chocolate to Keisha's eyes. Her mouth watered and she licked her lips. "I thought we would have some time together before you do business." She moved her hand across his chest before he could get his Sean John white T-shirt over his head to cover his body. Her lips were on his chocolate skin. He held the shirt in his hand and braced his back on the door. Keisha released his buckle and took his manhood in her mouth. Bling's eyes rolled back in his head. Keisha took in all of him and he grabbed her head.

Bang, bang. Someone pounded on the door. "Bling, open the door. Let's go. Time is money!"

Bling tried to free himself from Keisha but she still held on to him. "Give me a minute!" he shouted back. Keisha pulled her skirt up and turned her ass to him, letting him know that she wanted him. Bling couldn't resist. "Are you all right in there? Open the door," Bling's friend, Future, said.

Keisha wanted his friend to hear him loving her body. She was throwing it at him. She bent down and grabbed her ankles and he went wild. He couldn't control himself. He was giving it to her and she loved it. "It's all yours, baby. Give it to mama." Keisha knew her dirty talk would have him going wild and it worked.

"Do your thing, man!" Future yelled from outside the door. "I'll be in the lobby waiting."

After Bling left she took a short nap. She woke up and was upset at herself for wasting time sleeping when she could be enjoying paradise. She couldn't just stay in the room all day. Keisha unzipped her suitcase and found her leopard-print bikini. Keisha made her way to the beach with a white sheer sarong blowing in the wind. She found her spot on the beach and spread her towel. She sat for a few, taking in the beautiful scenery. The water was so inviting she couldn't deprive herself another minute. She pinned her hair up and took off her sarong and ran to greet the water.

***

The night of the show Keisha was indecisive about what outfit she would wear. Bling was getting irritable because he was one of the early performers and he didn't want to be late. "I told you what time we had to leave and you're still not dressed!"

Keisha took off the shirt she had just put on and was attempting to put on another. "Just give me a few more minutes. I want to look my best."

Bling flipped through the TV channels, not interested in anything that was on. "If Future gets here and you are not dressed, I'm leaving. Damn women can never get dressed on time."

She finally settled with a blouse that plunged all the way to her belly button, with the back plunging all the way to reveal the butterfly tattoo on her lower back. She paired it with jeans that had rips and cuts all over. Her black Gucci heels made the look complete. "How do I look?" She turned, facing Bling.

Bling was upset at how long it took her to get ready but he felt proud when he saw the final result. He knew she would look good on his arm. "You look like a million bucks." He nodded in approval.

"That's all?" Keisha wrinkled her brow.

There was a knock at the door and Bling jumped up to get it. "What's up, dawg?" he greeted his friend Future.

"You ready to put on a show?" Future asked as he greeted him.

"You know it."

Future looked past him and saw Keisha. "Who dat, my youth?" he whispered in his Jamaican accent.

"Keisha, let's go!" Bling ordered.

"Let me get my purse." She got her black and silver purse off the bed and did her runway walk to the door.

Future was smitten by her but he wouldn't dare cross the line. "I have to call my cousin to meet me at the show."

"If you are not in the lobby in five minute consider yourself left," Bling warned.

"She could use my phone. Just in case her cousin is fine she could save my number."

"You're always scheming." Bling shook his head.

"Look who is talking playa, playa."

They arrived at the show and headed backstage. The area was a little crowded. Artists were doing their ritual of smoking weed, which was their natural medicine. A few other artists had their woman with them and some were getting last-minute touchups by their stylists.

"Wha gwan, my youth?" was the greeting Bling received as he walk past his acquaintances. Keisha knew most of the artists from seeing their videos and from shows she went to and seen them perform at. Keisha was Jamaica but she has been living in the States ever since she was five years old. That was how she developed her go-getter attitude and always dressed to impress. It was the Jamaican motto.

Bling sat on a chair and Keisha sat on his lap. Bling knew that he had to show ownership of Keisha because the minute he turned his back someone would move in for the kill.

Through puffs of smoke Keisha could see wandering eyes scoping her out. It was getting humid backstage and she wished Bling was next on stage so they could leave to get back to the comfort of the hotel room. She was also looking forward to see her cousin, whom she hadn't seen in a few years. She didn't have enough time to visit her family while she was here but she knew she could count on her cousin to come visit her.

Future's phone was ringing and he answered it. "Hello." Keisha was listening to every word he said. "Yuh can't call mi phone and ask who dis." He hissed through his teeth.

Keisha got up and walked over to Future. "I think that's my cousin looking for me."

Future passed the phone to her. "She better look good."

"She's outside; how is she going to get in?"

"Future, just go escort the woman in," Bling ordered.

"She better look damn good." Future walked off.

"Her name is Tara!" Keisha yelled out to him, figuring he would need her name to know who she was. "What the hell is his problem?"

"Don't pay him any mind; that's how Future is."

Future escorted her cousin backstage and Keisha ran to her. "Hi, cousin!" Tara said in excitement. Nikki brought her over to Bling and introduced them.

"Bling, you're up next!" a voice announced. Bling made his way on stage.

Keisha and Tara caught up on each other's lives until they were interrupted by a well-known artist. "Why don't you take my number and call me tonight." He spoke directly to Keisha.

"I know you saw me with Bling."

"Bling is a small fry compare to me. Mi money nuff!"

Keisha walked away from him to an area where she could see Bling's performance.

"I will take his number if you don't want to," Tara announced.

"But he didn't want you," Keisha insulted her.

The weekend went by so fast. She wished she had one more night in paradise. But Bling had to return home to attend the recognition dinner her uncle was throwing in honor of his artist. She wished he would forget about his wife and bring her as his woman. She felt like Bling was hers to keep. She didn't want to give him back. She would hear him talking on his phone and she knew he was talking to his wife. But Keisha was the one in his bed so it didn't matter to her. His wife was the one being lied to, not her. But for now Keisha was his wife until he was away from her.

The final night in Jamaica together Keisha went all out. She showed him all her tricks. She didn't want him to forget about her. She wanted him to think of her when he went back to his wife. She wanted Bling to call out her name when she was making love to her. She wanted him to see her face whenever he said "I love you" to his wife.

Bling was also enjoying the fact the he was now an artist and could live his life like a rock star. They spent most of the weekend getaway indoors. Nothing could separate them from the bedroom. Keisha spent the final night sleeping in his arms, dreading that tomorrow they would have to part. This was the only other man Keisha was interested in for his heart, not his pocket.

A little after she had run away from home, she got married to the man she thought would love her for life, until she found out that he cheated on her a few months after the wedding with his ex. She vowed never again to love another man but to take them for whatever she could get. And that's how it'd been, until now. She was falling in love with Bling and she couldn't deny it.

The plane landed and they knew that they had to separate at the airport. Keisha despised having to walk behind him like a stranger as if they didn't know each other. She hated the fact that his wife usually volunteered to pick him up from the airport whether he wanted her to or not. Bling gave Keisha a tight embrace and she didn't want to let go.

"Honey!" He heard his wife's voice calling for him.

He quickly released Keisha. "My album will be out soon. Show your support!" He dismissed Keisha like one of his fans.

Keisha walked away, disgusted. His wife ran into his arms and Keisha witnessed their embrace. "Can you smell me on him, bitch?" She stood from a distance and watched them. There was no denying that's where Bling's heart was and she was envious. Keisha felt like no woman should come before her and his wife was definitely the frontrunner. At first Bling was just a business arrangement with her uncle, and the deal was already sealed, but she was now on a mission of her own to make Bling forget that he was a married man.

Bling glanced over his shoulder to locate Keisha. His eyes met her piercing stare, but he turned his attention back to his wife before his wife became suspicious. There was something about Keisha that he couldn't get enough of. It was like a magnetic force that kept pulling them together and drifting his attention away from his wife.

Keisha turned to walk away, not noticing the luggage that was next to her. She almost tripped but she quickly caught her balance. Keisha went outside and Hype was patiently waiting for her, leaning against his car. Hype was infatuated with her, so he was perfect for her little plan.

Patrick was having an artist appreciation dinner for his artists but she wasn't invited. He didn't want his secret weapon to be seen at his events and to have anyone connect the dots. Keisha felt that she should be at the event because if it weren't for her, he wouldn't have signed his two hottest artists right now. Besides, she wasn't going to do any more undercover work for her uncle because her main focus was Bling. But Hype was going to be her arm candy at this event and hopefully she could make Bling jealous.

"Come to papa," Hype said as he stretched his arms forward, waiting for her to run to him.

Instead she quick step past him. "Open the truck." Keisha put her shades on, blocking her eyes from the sun. She wore a long, flowing skirt with a tight-fitted blouse showing her belly. The wind blew slightly, making her skirt sway with the motion as if she were a Hawaiian hula dancer.

"Hello to you too!" He took the bag from her and she proceeded to open the passenger door and plant herself in the seat. "What's your problem? I was expecting a better greeting than this."

"I'm just a little jetlagged that's all." She had Hype wrapped around her little finger tighter than a sewn-in weave. She made him promise not to discuss their friendship with anyone, because he was a young tyrant who needed bragging rights. Secondly, she didn't want her double dipping to come to light because Keisha knew she was playing with fire. Hype was nothing but an extracurricular activity. He was more like a fun little puppy that you try to teach new tricks.

"Didn't you say tomorrow was the artist appreciation dinner? Will you be attending?" she asked with her ulterior motive.

"Yes. If the big man wants to acknowledge the work I'm doing I have to show my face," he said with a cocky attitude.

"Aren't you the big man? A recognition dinner just for you," Keisha said sarcastically.

"A few others will be mentioned too. So did you change your mind about accompanying me?"

"Since you made it crystal clear that this dinner is in celebration of you, why I would want to miss it?" Keisha knew her uncle would be upset with her but working for him was a wrap.

Hype placed his hand on her leg, feeling confident. He was going to be seen with this beautiful woman on his arm. "I'll have my stylist pick up a few dresses for you."

"You are too kind."

"You are my queen and my queen deserves the best."

She wanted to be with Bling at this very moment. But for now she had to compete with his wife and she knew it would be a strong competition. But Keisha knew that she lacked the skills to keep him satisfied and that was Keisha's biggest strength. Keeping a man happy in the bedroom was her forte.

Keisha got home and her driveway was blocked off by a moving truck. The back was open, exposing furniture and boxes. "What the hell is this?"

Hype couldn't put the car in park fast enough before Keisha got out of the car, hollering at the man blocking her driveway. "You are blocking my damn driveway!"

"You have to take that up with the lady of the house."

"I'm the lady of this damn house. You need to unblock my driveway."

Nikki and Tina came outside, carrying boxes with the word BREAKABLE written in bold letters. The look on Keisha face was priceless. She was unaware that Nikki had intentions of moving out.

"You are an ungrateful bitch! After all that I did for you?"

"Aren't you tired of singing the same old song?" Nikki passed the box to the mover and he took it to the back of the truck.

Nikki went back into the house and Keisha went after her with claws out, reminding her of everything she ever did for her as Nikki gathered the rest of her belongings. "I'll live to see you regret choosing Mark over me!"

Nikki was taken aback by the comment and paused to process what she just heard.

"If you honestly think that he loves you, you are even more delusional than I thought."

"Delusional. You need to get a fucking grip. You need to understand that I run my life, not you. You are just mad because you won't be able to put your nose in my business anymore."

"So all of a sudden you can pay your own rent?"

"Not that it's any of your damn business, but Mark is going to take care of that."

"Mark? On a cable guy salary?" She laughed. "Oh, I forgot you have no taste for luxury."

"Yes. Mark. He loves me, despite what you think of him." Nikki walked past Keisha and headed outside, but Keisha was hot on her trail.

"Why are you so interested in Nikki's life?" Tina chimed in.

"What are you even doing here?" she lashed out at Tina.

"I'm helping her move away from your crazy ass just in case you haven't noticed."

"So all of a sudden both of you grew balls. But both of you will come knocking at my damn door."

"I highly doubt it." Nikki got in her car and Keisha power-walked to her window.

"Aren't you forgetting something?"

"Are you really expecting me to say good-bye?"

"No, bitch. I'm expecting my damn keys back."

"I'm one step ahead of you. Check the garbage."

"You will get what's coming to you!" Keisha bellowed a loud, daunting laugh. It was as if she were possessed by demons. Tina knew nothing good could possibly come from that.

Tina was confused as to why Keisha was so interested in Nikki's relationship with Mark. She came to the conclusion that Keisha might be jealous of Nikki, but why should she be? Keisha could have had anybody she wanted. It was mindboggling to Tina.

"She is just setting herself up for a fall. I can't believe she can't see through his lies," Keisha ranted.

"Whose lies? What lies, and what are you talking about? When others are doing well, you see it as a threat, and instead of commending them you find ways to keep them down so you will always be on top," Tina defended Nikki.

Deep inside Keisha knew that she was the problem. Nikki was accomplishing the things that her parents wanted for her and deep inside she was disappointed in herself. But she put up a front to hide her true feelings. Keisha didn't respond to Tina. She picked up her bag and went inside.

Chapter 15

Mark sat outside Nikki's new apartment, awaiting Nikki's arrival. She was delighted to see him and gladly ran into his arms. Mark found her a cozy one-bedroom apartment on the other side of town. He wanted her away from Keisha and that's exactly what he did. The neighborhood wasn't spectacular but the apartment was newly refurbished. She exhaled deeply, releasing all the negative energy that had consumed her before stepping into her new apartment.

"Welcome home, baby. It's just me and you." Mark led her to the carpeted, unfurnished living room and she was startled. He had set up a picnic in the center of the floor. "This is all for you." He surprised her with her favorite chicken salad and a bottle of champagne. He also had a few balloons with the words WELCOME HOME written on them.

Thank you, God, for sending me my Mr. Right, and if I am dreaming, God, please don't make me wake up. "You are full of surprises. I wonder what else you have up your sleeves."

Mark lifted her off her feet then walked over to the festivity he had set up for her. "This is how a real man treats a lady." He popped the champagne bottle open and it sprayed everywhere. Nikki shielded her face with her hands.

Mark's phone started to ring in his pocket. He handed the bottle to Nikki and forced his hand inside his fitted

jean pocket and retrieved his phone. He viewed the
number but ignored the call.

"Here you go, baby." Nikki handed him the glass.

"Cheers to your new home."

Nikki paused before drinking. "Cheers to our new
home. That's more like it." Mark's phone started to ring
again and he handed his glass to Nikki and proceeded to
the door. "Where are you going?" she questioned.

"I'll be right back. What is it!" he answered, closing the
door behind him.

It was obvious that the person on the other end wasn't
someone he wanted to engage in a conversation with.
Nikki peeked out the window. She could see him pacing
back and forth with his mouth saying a million words per
minute. She could tell he was upset at whoever he was
speaking with. His mannerisms made Nikki question his
character because she never saw him this upset before.
She couldn't hear what he was saying because he was on
the opposite side of the street.

Mark was making his way back and Nikki ran from the
window and assumed her position on the floor, eating
her salad. Before Mark could get both his feet in the door
Nikki wanted answers. "What was that about?"

"That was my sister running her mouth about putting
my mother in a nursing home because she has no time to
take care of her."

*I don't know what I was expecting him to say but to
know that he is concerned about his mother makes him
more of a gentleman to me.* "I dread getting old," Nikki
stated.

"My sister is just ungrateful, that's all."

Mark finished his glass of champagne and poured
himself another and finished it quickly. Nikki watched
him intently, with the fork halfway to her mouth.

"I have to leave town tomorrow to go help her out for
a few days."

"Where does your sister live?" Nikki was curious.

Mark answered the question with a question of his own. "So did your roommate give you a sendoff party?"

Nikki rolled her eyes. "More like a kick in the ass out the door. I think she was behind all the unexplainable events that happened while I was in that house."

"What are you talking about?"

"I would pick out an outfit for work and a mysterious stain would appear in the morning."

"What are you saying?" Mark raised the glass to his head.

"The other day I was looking for my book and I know I left it on the table but it wasn't there when I returned. Do you know where I found it?"

"Let me guess: it was taped to the ceiling." Mark laughed at his own sarcasm.

"This isn't funny, Mark." The fork was carrying another piece of chicken to her mouth.

"Okay, okay. Where was it?"

"No, it was in the damn garbage!"

"How the hell did it get there?"

"That's the same question I asked myself and now I know it was Keisha."

"Do you really—"

"Who else would it be?"

"That girl is out to get you and you need to stay away from her. Trust me, she is evil."

The fork was now resting on her plate. "You speak as if you know her personally."

"Let's not talk about Keisha right now." He got up and walked to the fridge and got the ice cream. "Let's think about all the places on your body I'm going to put this ice cream."

"How about here?" She touched her neck.

"I was thinking someplace else." He kissed her passionately while using his finger to spoon the ice cream and raised it to her mouth. Nikki lengthened her tongue and licked the ice cream from his fingers. She moaned, letting him know she was enjoying the foreplay.

"Baby, I love you," she said aloud. It was the first time Mark was hearing those words from her and he now more than ever wanted her to experience real pleasure. "I want to feel you inside me, baby," she said. .

Mark entered her and she wrapped her legs around him. He gave her all his manhood and she moaned with each stroke. They climaxed together and there was no denying that the neighbors now knew their names.

It was eight p.m. when Mark woke up. Nikki's arms were wrapped around him so he slowly removed himself from her grip, not wanting to wake her. Mark turned, facing her, and her naked body greeted his eyes. His manhood hardened in his boxers but he had to deny himself. He rummaged through the unpacked boxes and found a sheet to cover her chocolate brown skin. Mark took his jeans off the floor and his buckle rattled, causing Nikki to stir in her sleep. Mark paused for a moment, then proceeded getting dressed after she was settled. Mark tiptoed to the door and gently closed the door behind him.

It was seven o'clock in the morning when Nikki woke up, hoping to see Mark next to her. "How about bringing me breakfast in bed? I mean on the floor." Nikki turned to face Mark but he wasn't there. Thinking that he was in the kitchen she dragged her feet, still worn out from last night. "Babes, I don't smell any pancakes or eggs." Mark wasn't in the kitchen.

"Are you in the bathroom?" Her steps quickened. "I would love to take a shower with you." She pushed the door open but the shower wasn't running. "He probably went to get coffee." Nikki dialed Mark's number but she didn't get any answer so she left a message. "Can you make my coffee French vanilla with five sugars?"

To kill time she decided to unpack her clothes and bathroom products; then she took a shower. She wanted to be fresh and clean when Mark came home, just in case he wanted to have her for lunch.

Speaking of lunch it was almost twelve noon and he still wasn't back. "Where the hell is he?" Nikki redialed the number. "Where are you?" she demanded.

"I'm at my restaurant. I mean, I'm at my favorite restaurant, buying lunch. I didn't want to wake you when I left for work this morning."

"I totally forgot that you had work today. What time will you be home later?"

"I have to leave to go see my mother after work, remember? I'll call you later." He ended the call quickly.

Nikki removed the phone from her ear, viewing it as if it had a malfunction and Mark didn't just hang up on her.

Lately she has been so preoccupied with Mark that she forgot about studying. With no plans for the day she decided to pick up her books and do some catching up.

After an hour of studying Nikki couldn't keep her focus. Her mind kept drifting back to the night she just had with Mark. Her thoughts were discombobulated. She never thought she would fall in love with Mark but she could no longer deny that she was head over heels. "I should just surprise him at his job before he leaves." Nikki closed her book and hurry to get dressed and run to her car.

In no time she was pulling in the parking lot. She went inside and there were two people before her in line. Two receptionists were now available so she was next. "May I help you?" the grumpy receptionist asked.

"I was wondering if you could page Marcus," Nikki politely asked.

The receptionist looked confused. "There is no Marcus at this location."

"Marcus Gray," Nikki restated.

"Allan, did we get a new hire? This lady is looking for a Marcus," she yelled to the equipment room. A man walked up to the receptionist and whispered in her ear. The lady rolled her eyes and brought her attention to Nikki. "There is a Marcus at one of our other locations, but everyone is out in the field this time of the day. Call his cell phone next time. Next!" She dismissed Nikki.

She stepped aside and the next person in line bumped into her going to the window. "I think the words are 'excuse me,'" she said with an attitude.

"*Puta,*" the Spanish woman said, rolling her eyes.

Nikki went back to her car to retrieve her cell phone. She had one missed call from Mark. She pressed the button on her BlackBerry and dialed his number.

"Hey, baby," he answered. "I heard you went looking for me."

"That woman acted as if she didn't know who you are."

"She knows me well. She just wants a piece of me but she's mad 'cause you getting all of this." Nikki laughed. "I'm heading to the apartment right now to get some of that before I leave town."

"I'm on my way." Nikki hung up the phone and turned the key in the ignition and sped off to her apartment.

She slowed for a stop sign but didn't make a complete stop in her haste to get to Mark. But red and blue lights were hot on her tail.

"Damn." Nikki pounded her fist on the steering wheel. As she pulled over to the side of the road she was hoping the process didn't take long so she could be on her way home to Mark.

***

Mark got to the apartment and Nikki's car wasn't there. So he hurried inside because he wanted to surprise her when she walked in. He made a dash to the refrigerator and got the whipped cream. Mark stripped down to his birthday suit as he made his way back to the front door. When she walked in he wanted her to see him standing firm. He heard the sound of a car door closing and he hastily covered his manhood with the whipped cream. Mark closed his eyes and parted his legs, leaving his dick to hang. The person fumbled with lock as if she didn't have a key. *What the hell is taking her so long to open the door? Did she forget her key?* Mark suddenly felt the breeze from outside on his chest. He still remained with his eyes closed. He felt her hands crawling down his chest. "Yeah, baby. Make daddy happy."

"Meow," the voice whispered in his ear and the warmth of her breath made his dick jump. He felt her behind him. She reached around his body and grabbed his chest, holding him tight. "Keep your eyes closed," she whispered in his ear. She clawed his chest with her fingers.

"Damn, girl. I didn't know you were a wild kitten." She circled his nipples with her finger, sending chills through his body. "Why don't you put some whipped cream on them?" Mark ordered. He felt the cold whipped cream on his body and he twitched. "Let me feel your warm tongue on my body, baby," he begged. "Make big daddy happy."

"Why don't you keep your eyes closed and make mommy happy." The words whispered in his ear, sending chills down his body. Fffzzz. Ffzzz. The sound of whipped cream leaving the can had Mark anticipating her next move. "I like this. Why don't you put some whipped cream on your spot and let me go treasure hunting."

"What the hell is going on in here?" Nikki voice erupted when she opened the door.

Mark opened his eyes and beheld Nikki at the door. He looked above to see Keisha with a devious grin on her face, holding the whipped cream in her hand. "I thought . . . I thought . . . I thought it was you."

"You lying bastard!" Nikki ran toward him, wanting to kill him.

Keisha got out of the way and watched her pounce on him. "I hope you like your housewarming present. I told you I could have him if I wanted him."

Nikki made a U-turn and jumped on Keisha. Mark picked up his pants off the floor and hurriedly put his legs in. He picked Keisha up off Nikki and she let out the same wicked laugh like she did before. "Why would you do this to me?" Nikki charged at him and he held on to her.

"You have to listen to me. I honestly thought she was you."

"It's a damn shame you don't know what your woman feels like."

Nikki wanted to jump on her but Mark held her back. "Listen to me! Nikki, calm down. Why would I have her come here when I told you to meet me here? This bitch is crazy! She broke in the apartment. Nikki, I had my eyes closed thinking it was you!"

"He knew it was me and he enjoyed every minute of it."

"How did you know where I live?"

"Bitch, please. Do you honestly think that Tina would keep your secret?"

Mark turned Nikki to face him and looked deep into her eyes. "She just wants what you got!"

"I can have your man and you can't do anything about it," Keisha sang as she left.

"She is crazy, Nikki; you have to believe me." Mark kissed her lips and she slapped him so hard his head turned.

"You were just with that fucking whore! And you think you can put your lips on me?" Nikki ran to the bathroom and washed her mouth. Nikki knew Mark was telling the truth because he hadn't done anything suspicious before that would cause her to doubt his honesty. Keisha was vindictive and wasn't going to stop until she destroyed her relationship with Mark. Keisha was just jealous and she knew it.

Nikki locked herself in the bedroom and Mark could hear her crying. Even though she believed him the fact still remained that Keisha was too close for comfort. She was violated. After several attempts of pleading with her to open the door and she didn't, Mark decided to go and confront Keisha about her antics.

Mark slowed his speed when he neared Keisha's condo. He remembered the first time he met Nikki and how her fiery attitude had him wanting her. A wide smile invaded his lips as he relived the moment. He got closer to the house and a limo was park outside. A man dressed in a three-piece suit stood at her door. Mark stopped his car on the opposite side out of curiosity.

Keisha stepped out, looking extravagant. She wore a black formfitting long gown that she held with her left hand to avoid dragging it on the ground. The man reached for her hand and she extended her right arm. She needed the support because she was afraid of tripping in her six-inch silver Gucci heels. Tonight of all nights she didn't want to break her ankle and miss seeing the jealous wives' and groupies' envious stares when she made her grand entrance. She noticed Mark's car and flashed him a smile, knowing deep inside he wanted a piece of her.

Chapter 16

Keisha took a moment to reapply her lip gloss while Hype held the limo door open for her to exit. Hype was overjoyed to be accompanied to the artist appreciation dinner with such a beauty. He extended his arm and Keisha reached for it as she scooted out of the limo. Hype walked proudly with her on his arm but deep inside Keisha wished it were Bling instead of him.

Once inside they were escorted to a vacant table that was reserved for Hype and his guest. Bling's eyes popped open and he almost choked on the champagne that he had just sipped. Her uncle also stopped in mid speech because he too was caught off-guard. *What the hell is she thinking? She is supposed to be my undercover weapon.* Patrick cleared his throat and resumed his speech, welcoming Hype and his guest. Hype kissed Keisha's hand and the look on Bling's face was priceless.

Patrick acknowledged all his newly signed artists. Bling was sitting to his left and he raised his glass to him. Patrick gave a long speech about his vision for his company. He went on and on about the direction in which he wanted to take his artists, and then finally closed by also wishing them longevity in the business. "I would like to have all my artists on stage for a promotional photo," Patrick stated, raising his glass. The photographers snapped pictures from every angle. Keisha viewed the room and the other chairs were occupied by executives, promoters, and their dates—also groupies for hire.

Ten empty chairs made it clear for Keisha to see all the wives and girlfriends who came with an artist. *These bitches should view me as a threat because I can have their man if I wanted to.* Keisha did a double take when she spotted Bling's wife. She stood out from the rest of cheap knockoff dresses that decorated the room. Her dress was exquisite and she wore it well. Keisha wished she had lost her fashion sense that day when she picked it out thinking Bling was buying it for her.

Keisha turned her attention only to see Bling's eyes focused on her. Keisha blew him a kiss and Bling turned his head to see his wife staring at Keisha. Keisha followed Bling's eyes, and his wife's eyes cut her like a knife. They both held their stares, sizing up each other, until the waiter broke the staring contest when he walked over to refill Keisha's drink. Bling got back to his seat and kissed his wife on her cheek. "Who is that woman and why were you staring at her?" She quickly threw out the question at Bling.

"She just resembled someone I once knew," he lied.

Patrick's voice interrupted the multiple conversations in the room. "Can I have everyone's attention? I would like to say drink all you can, eat all you can, but I'm expecting to see everyone in the studio bright and early tomorrow morning."

Patrick went over to Bling's table and introduced himself to his wife. He filled her in on how challenging it was to get Bling signed to his label. "I hope you had something to do with his sudden change of heart."

Bling look over at Keisha and Hype was all over her. Keisha was also putting on a show because she knew Bling was checking her out every chance he got and she wanted to make him jealous. The same annoying guy who was with Bling at the club the first night she met him came over to their table. Keisha had no idea that he was a washed-up artist whose career had flopped. He shook hands with Hype and he introduced him to Keisha.

"I know him," Keisha confessed quickly because she didn't want this guy to think was hiding anything. Hype looked at her as if searching for an answer. "I met this little annoying puppy at the club a while back."

"I see that you are still feisty as usual."

Keisha excused herself and headed to the ladies' room. Bling saw her leave and took it as his cue to follow her. He too excused himself and swiftly caught up with her in the hallway.

"What the hell is that about?" Bling yelled out to her in an aggressive tone.

Keisha recognized the voice but was a little unsure because she had just left him inside with his wife. She turned to face him.

"Why would you disrespect me like that?" Bling asked.

"You had me pick out your wife's dress; that's what I would call disrespectful. Showing up with another man is merely close in comparison."

"He is my label mate. Isn't that too close for comfort?"

"Is the heat in the kitchen is too hot for you? Besides, I owe you no explanation."

She walked away and he grabbed her arm. Bling seemed to have forgotten where he was and that he was with his wife. A waiter entered the hallway and he let go of her arm. The waiter went outside and Bling took her by her arm, leading her out of sight.

"You are a married man, or did you forget? Unless she can't satisfy you the way I do." She walked over to him, pushing him against the wall, and kissed him seductively. He tried to hold on to her but she walked away from him.

"I'm not going to be your mistress."

Keisha entered the ladies room. Bling went in after her, locking the door behind him.

"What are you doing? What about your wife?"

He pushed her against the door and kissed her seductively. She wanted him just as much as he wanted her but for a second she was curious about his wife. It wasn't a genuine concern. She just wanted to hear him say it was all about her.

"Let me worry about her. Right now I want you."

Hearing him say that fueled her deep desire for him. She forgot about Hype and they even forgot where they were. Bling lifted her dress and took her right there. Their chemistry was undeniable and even though it was wrong it felt right.

Just as their flame subsided there was a knock at the door and the lock was shaking. They remained completely quiet until they heard the footsteps walking away. Bling cracked the door and heard his wife asking if anyone knew where he was. It seemed as if everyone was now in the hallway because Hype made the statement that he was also missing his date. Bling came out of the bathroom and made his way to the door that exited outside without been seen. He reentered the main lobby, talking on his phone.

His wife spotted him and marched over, demanding an answer. "Where were you?"

"I couldn't get service on my phone so I went outside to make a call." Bling took her by her arm and led her back into the ballroom.

Hype and Keisha walked in, hand in hand, and approached Bling's table. Denise looked at her viciously in attack mode.

"I see you found your husband." Hype stated the obvious when he got to Bling's table.

"I could say the same to you," Bling's wife stated.

"This is Keisha, my date." Hype introduced her to Bling and his wife not knowing a storm was brewing. "Keisha, this is Bling. You already know he's one of the artists on the label."

Keisha shook his hand as if this were the first time they ever touched. Bling also introduced his wife. "This is my wife, Denise, the love of my life." Bling kissed Denise on her cheek; and Keisha hugged Hype around his waist for support because she was sick to her stomach, but she couldn't help herself from taking jabs at Denise.

"I see the love, but aren't you worried when he's on tour with all these women wanting a piece of him?"

"I have faith in my husband."

"You really have her trained to say the right things in public."

"And who are you again other than Hype's arm candy?"

Patrick came over and introduced a representative from a magazine company who wanted to interview both of the guys. It was a real icebreaker. Denise stared at Keisha like a lioness ready to protect her territory.

On the ride home that night Hype was all over her but the only man she wanted was Bling; but not knowing what lay ahead for her and Bling was frustrating. All she knew was that she wanted him to herself.

Her cell phone rang and she quickly opened her purse to get it. She needed a distraction from Hype breathing all over her, so a conversation with her worst enemy would have been accepted. She saw the name Bling and she was in heaven. "Hello," she said anxiously. But the conversation on the other end wasn't directed at her. Bling's phone had dialed her number by accident.

"I love you so much," his wife said, and Keisha cringed at the sound of her voice.

"I love you too," Bling replied. Keisha wanted to puke.

"Baby, I have good news." Keisha pressed the phone on her ear, not wanting to miss a word.

"Are you going to tell me or what?" Keisha rolled her eyes.

"I think I might be pregnant."

"What?" Keisha yelled into the phone in unison with Bling.

"Is everything okay?" Hype asked.

"Yes. It's just Nikki being a drama queen as usual.

"We might finally have the family we always wanted. Aren't you happy?" his wife continued.

"I thought you were on the pill," Bling questioned.

The limo went under an overpass and Keisha lost the signal. "Damn!" She was pissed because she wouldn't hear the end of the conversation. *Does he want to have a baby with his wife? Is he mad at her for not being on the pill? If she is pregnant do I stand a chance with Bling?*

The limo stopped at her gate and Hype opened the door.

"Tonight was lovely. I would invite you in but I'm so tired. I'll call you in the morning," Keisha quickly rejected him, and hurried to the door with her keys in hand. She tried to put the key in door but the door opened on its own. *What the fuck? Maybe I didn't fully close it when I left.* She remembered Bling saying someone had tampered with the lock the last time he stopped by. Keisha viewed the lock but it was intact. "Not my damn jewelry!" she yelled.

She swung the door open and the smell of burning cigarettes consumed her nostrils, which was quite unusual. She kicked her shoes off and turned her nose up and sniffed, following the scent like a hound dog on a trail. The scent got stronger as she approached the living room. A small, circular orange flame brightened in the dark living room. Keisha heart was pulsating fast like the beat of a reggae song as the silhouette of a man walked toward her. She nervously turned the light switch on, revealing that the person was Mark.

"What are you doing in my house?"

"Look who the cat dragged in." He blew the smoke in her face. She reached up to slap him but he grabbed her arm. Mark was six feet in height and towered over her. "You need to stay away from Nikki."

"And if I don't?"

"You don't want to know the answer to that. But consider it a warning." Mark released his grip and walk away from her.

"You broke my damn lock! You better fix it."

"I can't take credit for that. It's was open when I got here." Mark exited the house knowing he delivered his message loud and clear.

Keisha closed the door behind him and was startled to death when she turned and saw Johnny standing before her. She braced herself against the door so she wouldn't collapse. It was now obvious that Johnny was the one who broke into her apartment. Johnny had obviously been hiding in her apartment for the entire time. *Was Mark in on this too?*

"You need to crawl back through the hole you crawled in from before I call the police and let them know that an infectious creature had escaped the zoo." Keisha was unsure of what to make of this stunt Johnny was pulling. She also felt fear blanketing her body but she dared not let him see the fear in her eyes.

"You need to adjust your insults, because just in case you didn't notice I'm in charge."

"You need to get the hell out my apartment!"

Johnny punched the wall and his fist went through. Keisha tried to run past him but he grabbed her arm. "I need you. I want you to love me."

Keisha wiggled her arm in an attempt to get away. "Let go of my arm! You are hurting me."

He pulled her close to him and planted his lips on hers. Keisha kicked him in his balls and he let go of her. She ran to her bedroom and closed the door. She franticly dialed Bling's phone but it went straight to voicemail. She was calling him again when Johnny kicked the door in. Johnny charged at her like a madman.

"I'm calling the police!" she screamed at him. He picked her up off her feet and tossed her on the bed. She was horrified to see Johnny on top of her.

"Get off me! What are you doing?" He forcefully tried to kiss her and she turned her head from side to side to avoid his filthy mouth. She punched him in his eye and he rolled off her, holding his eye. Keisha tried to run but her feet became tangled in her long dress, bringing her to the ground.

"Come here. I'm going to treat you like the bitch you really are."

"Your brother showed you who the real bitch was when he ran off with your whore of a wife."

That struck a nerve with Johnny. Johnny had become a monster. He had warned her that she would regret the way she treated him. Johnny had been secretly watching her every move. He had become obsessed with Keisha but now he had allowed his anger to get the best of him. "You are ruining my dress!"

"You already ruined it. Only you could manage to cheapen an expensive dress."

It was only Keisha who would be worried about a dress at a time like this. She spit in his face and the back of his hand hit her face, causing her to let out a loud scream. A single tear ran down her left cheek. Johnny wiped it with his index finger then licked it. He saw the fear in Keisha's eyes and he giggled. "If you weren't so damn busy hurling insults when I come around, you would know what true love really is. I'm always trying to get you to notice me."

"Someone help me please!" She was fighting with him. But he overpowered her. He was lifting her dress and ripping it in the process. "You will regret this!"

"Only if it's not what I expect it to be."

Keisha fought with all her might. Her energy was low. She couldn't prevent Johnny from entering her and he tackled her body like a wild animal. She fantasized about Bling coming to save her. Her fantasy didn't come to reality because Bling couldn't hear her cry. He couldn't feel her pain. He didn't and he couldn't. She couldn't move. Her brain wouldn't signal to her legs to move because she was lost in disbelief.

Johnny got to his climax and laid his body lifelessly on top of her. She felt his heart pounding like a drum. "You need to start doing your Kegel exercises. Woman, thou art loose," he said, rolling off of her. Her body felt paralyzed. Even though the ordeal was over she lay there in disbelief.

Johnny fixed himself and took out his wallet, tossing a dollar bill at her. He left her crying on the floor. The door slammed shut behind Johnny and Keisha jumped at the sound. Her body quivered on the floor as she cried like a baby.

Hours had passed and she remained in the same spot. She finally got herself together and tried to get up, holding on to the wall for support, but her legs got weak and she fell to the floor. She dragged herself to the bathroom where she saw her reflection in the mirror. She took a step back and looked at the person she didn't recognized. Her hair resembled a bird's nest and her face was stained with two lines indicating where her tears had traveled down her face while crying. Her eyes were swollen and her face was bruised from his abuse. Tears slowly trickled down her face as she relived the ordeal she had endured. She made a loud scream like a wounded animal. He had violated her. She turned the shower on to its full force, letting the water beat her skin as she tried to wash him off her body.

After her long, hot shower that seemed like forever, she climbed into bed, but she couldn't rest peacefully. Every time she closed her eyes the flashback of Johnny raping her made her cringed. She sobbed into her pillow uncontrollably.

Keisha wasn't going to let Johnny get away with raping her. He had to pay for what he did and she wanted him to pay with his life. She remembered that she had her cell phone in her purse. She ran to the living room and saw her purse on the couch. She hastily opened her purse but her phone battery was dead. The phone met the wrath of Keisha when it landed into the wall and the battery flew across the room. "You will pay for this! You will pay for this!"

She dropped herself onto the floor, pulling her knees into her chest, cuddling herself for comfort. She was alone and vulnerable. She wanted Bling to rescue her. She wanted to be loved by him. Behind the tough girl image she had perfected all she really wanted was to be kissed on the inside.

Chapter 17

Keisha didn't and couldn't fall asleep. Her eyes were getting heavy but she feared closing them because the ordeal of Johnny raping her would come rushing back clear as day. The doorbell chimed and she rocked herself back and forth, blocking out the disturbance of the never-ending chimes.

The house phone started to ring and she covered her ears. "Leave me alone. Leave me alone!" The machine picked up.

"I know you said you were tired last night but I'm hoping you would let me in this morning. I just want to talk for a few before I go to the studio. I'm at the door; let me in."

She started to hum, still cuddling herself.

"Come on, Keisha, open the door! Let me know if you are okay. You better be because I would kill anybody if they hurt my queen."

Keisha's eyes opened wide. Hype had said exactly what she wanted to hear. She was thinking of a way to eliminate Johnny and Hype was the perfect man for the job. She ran to the door and held him tight. He had to take a step back to balance himself.

"You can't let him get away with this." She repeated those words over and over as she sobbed on his arm.

Hype was confused as to what she was talking about until he raised her head and he saw her face. "Who did this to you?"

She spared him the details of Johnny raping her because she didn't want him to view her any differently, like she was damaged goods. She filled him in on how he abused her because he was obsessed. She wanted him dead and just the mere fact that he had hurt her was reason enough for him to go after Johnny.

"I'm going to kill him. Look what he did to you. Where can I find him?"

"42 Wood Lawn Avenue." Hype was about to walk away but Keisha stopped him. "I have a picture of him on my phone." She went to the bedroom and retrieved her charger and plugged it in. She scanned through her pictures, shielding the phone from Hype. "Here he is." She showed the picture to Hype without letting him get a hold of her phone. She did want him to scan through it and see her picture with Bling.

It was a picture of him with his arms around Tina. Hype sealed the image of Johnny in him memory and hastily walked to the door. "Be careful!" Keisha ran behind him. Hype kissed her forehead and left. If Hype couldn't do the job she was going to do it herself. It wouldn't be a hard task to get Johnny. All she had to do was convince him that she enjoyed him so much she wanted more and he would come running. Then she would cut his dick off and watch him bleed to death.

Keisha went from room to room cleaning and organizing. She tried to keep herself busy so she wouldn't think about last night.

Several hours elapsed and Hype hadn't called. She wanted to know what had happened. She stared at the clock, and seconds turned into minutes, and minutes into hours. The kitchen, bathroom, bedrooms, and every crevice and corner were spotless. Her closet was the next place she organized. Her walk-in closet was like a department store itself. Keisha rearranged her colors from dark to light. Her eyes were tired and she was about to fall asleep standing but she was trying desperately to keep them open.

Ding-dong. The doorbell startled her. She ran to the door and looked out the peephole and saw that it was Hype standing there. "What took you so long?" She pulled him inside.

"It took me awhile to locate him; besides, I had to do the job right."

She showered him with barrage of questions. "Did you wear gloves? Did you leave any evidence behind? Did anyone see you?" She didn't stop for him to answer the first or second question before asking another.

He placed his finger on her lips. "The murder would be an unsolved mystery. That's all I have to say."

For two weeks Keisha put herself under house arrest, cutting off the outside world, including Bling. She didn't want to show that her beauty was now disfigured from a rapist gone mad because beauty to her was on the outside. She had summoned Hype to run her errands, so he had now become a frequent guest. They had developed a closer bond in her time of need. But still Bling was in her every thought. To avoid Bling coming around she told him she had left town on a job assignment. She needed Hype at the moment to do her dirty work, nothing more, nothing less.

Her head was rested in Hype's lap when breaking news flashed on the flat-screen seventy-two-inch TV. The news reporter's makeup was overdone. Even her lipstick wasn't the right shade for her.

"A man was found dead in a Dumpster by a homeless man searching for food early this morning. The identity of the man is unknown and with his head, fingers, toes, and genitalia missing he will remain unidentified unless the killer comes forward."

She knew it was Johnny because Hype had told her how he begged for his life as he slowly cut off his body parts. She excitedly pounced on Hype, showing her gratitude.

"He didn't deserve to live after what he did to you. You are my queen and no one should treat you less."

Feeling inspired to write his music Hype anxiously departed to meet up with his label mates at the studio. Feeling justified in her action, showing no remorse or grief, she celebrated with a glass of her favorite red wine with a toast to Johnny.

"And I will be at your funeral to spit on your damn grave."

Chapter 18

Nikki threw up her scrambled eggs and orange juice she had for breakfast. She thought she had a stomach virus and didn't bother to second-guess herself the first few mornings it happened. But this morning right on time as she finished her breakfast her guts were coming up. *I can't be pregnant.*

Nikki remembered when she was unpacking her feminine products there was a pregnancy test that she undoubtedly knew belonged to Keisha. Nikki ran to the linen closet and rummaged through her box of sanitary items. *Bingo!* She ran back to the bathroom, leaving the linen closet door open. She quickly peed on the stick, wetting her hand in the process. She didn't read the instructions; she just knew she had to pee on it.

"Was I supposed to soak it like this?" Nikki wrapped the dripping stick in some tissue and placed it on the sink. She washed her hands, eyeing the test. The minute couldn't come fast enough. Nikki paced back and forth, now holding the test in her hand. The positive sign appeared and she was flabbergasted at the result, dropping the test on the floor. Her scream echoed throughout the house. "This can't be happening." Nikki was now hyperventilating. Tears ran down her face because she knew deep down she wasn't ready for this.

"No. No!" She pounded the door with her fist. After several minutes she gathered herself, walking out the bathroom to retrieve her cell phone. She hadn't spoken to Mark since the incident but this was reason enough to call him. Mark answered his phone. Nikki was on the verge of tears. "I need you to come by the house now."

"I'll be there in a minute," Mark replied without hesitation.

"This can't be happening! This can't be happening."

Within minutes Mark was at the door. "Nikki, where are you?" he called out as he entered. "I'm glad you came to your senses and realize you need me in your life."

Nikki came out to meet him and he walked over quickly to embrace her. "Why are you crying? I honestly didn't mean to hurt you. You have to believe me. I didn't know that it was her."

Mark hugged her and Nikki sobbed in his arms. "I promise I'll make it up to you. Look at me." He held her up to view her face.

"Mark, I'm pregnant!"

He quickly released his grip, placing his hand on his head. "You can't be. Aren't you suppose to be on the damn pill?" Mark scratched his head.

"Yes, but I missed a few last month."

"How could you be so damn careless?"

His reaction threw her off. The words that were coming out of his mouth weren't what she expected to hear. "Careless?" Nikki repeated.

"What do you intend to do?" he asked, walking away from her.

"We have to get married," she declared. "I can't have a baby out of wedlock. I can't have a child and not be married. It just can't happen."

"What are you talking about, marriage?" He turned to face her. "You can't keep this baby. You need to make an appointment for an abortion."

Nikki's five fingers were printed on his face before he could say another word. Nikki was stunned at his response. She knew that she wasn't ready for a baby. But it was disturbing to know that he wanted her to abort her child.

"You females are always trying to trap a man. I'm not ready for a baby and that's my final word."

"Get out! Get the hell out of my apartment."

Mark left the house, slamming the door behind him. Nikki fell to the floor, sobbing.

For months Nikki was living in a bubble, overjoyed and in love. She was blinded by the idea of love and all the amenities that came with it. Her life revolved around Mark. She believed in his every word like it was her daily bread. No logical thinking was coming from her brain. The only things she uttered were, "Mark said this," and "Mark said that." It's like she was brainwashed. The man who stood before her and told her to have an abortion was someone she didn't know.

Chapter 19

Today was the day Keisha would take her life back. Johnny was dead and she was no longer going to let the bruises he put on her face keep her home. Besides, today was his funeral and she was going to show her last respects. Johnny's mother had identified the body after recognizing his clothes. "My son was harmless. He didn't hurt a soul. Who would do this to my boy?" she'd hollered on the news.

"Your precious boy hurt this woman and that was a big mistake, big mistake!" Keisha shouted at the TV, hoping the old woman would hear her.

Her M·A·C makeup applied heavily covered her bruised face. The cherry red Chanel pantsuit in the back of her closet had been waiting for the right occasion and the time was now. She was going to bring some fire to his funeral. She got to the door but detoured to get the dress that she had on the night Johnny had raped her. She was planning on leaving it on his casket at the church after she spit on it. As she put the dress in the black garbage bag she was fueled with anger and rage as she power-walked to the front door. Hype made it his priority to fix the lock and she double-checked, making sure she closed it behind her.

She unlocked her car and gracefully entered. She reversed out her driveway but quickly jammed on her brakes to avoid hitting a dog. She got to the parking lot of the New Testament Church of God in less than ten minutes, and as usual it was packed with cars. *What a joke. Johnny only went to church to steal from the damn offering plate.* Keisha remembered the exact words he said to her. *I just want to get closer to the offering plate; church is where the money is. Do you see the car the pastor is driving? I see people playing the lotto but church is where I'm going to hit the jackpot.*

Keisha decided to double park and blocked Pastor Blake Bentley. He wasn't going anywhere soon and besides she wasn't staying long. When she entered the church two ushers looked at her with a dirty frown. "Are you aware that you do not wear red to a funeral?" one lady said as the other looked her up and down.

Keisha paused with her hands on her hips. "Well, this is a party for me. I'm celebrating the fact that he's dead."

The ladies gasped. Keisha walked right by them. Pastor Blake was preaching about the importance of repentance. Keisha walked up the aisle, listening to whispers and sighs as she passed each row of seats. The pastor stopped in midsentence, trying to figure out who this lady was. "This is a funeral precession, young lady. If you need prayer I'll meet with you after the service."

Keisha ignored him as she untied the knot in the trash bag. She spread the dress over the casket then spit on it. "Go to hell. You bastard!"

You could hear the loud gasp from the mourners. "Get her out of here!" A woman in a wide-brim black hat, also wearing all black cover from head-to-toe, sitting in the front seat jumped to her feet. "My boy was a loving man. He doesn't deserve to be disrespected!"

Keisha faced the elderly woman. "Your loving son raped me! He deserved to die!"

The woman slapped Keisha's face and she held her burning cheek. Keisha turned and spat on the coffin again. And once again the mourners gasped. "I hope the devil rides him like a horse in hell!"

"Get this woman out of this church!" Pastor Blake yelled. A few family members and ushers rushed to get her out of the church.

"Don't touch me! I know my way out."

They followed her until she exited the church. Keisha made it a point of duty to leave a dent in the pastor's Bentley.

Chapter 20

"No! This can't be happening."

Nikki was on her way to her car when she detoured and ran back inside. Her head was in the bowl, hurling up everything in her stomach. "I have to take my finals," she said, wiping her mouth. Morning sickness was getting the best off her. She slowly stood to her feet, holding her stomach. "Why is this happening to me?" She looked at herself in the mirror and tears ran from her eyes. Today was the last day to make up her exam. For the past three days she tried putting one foot out the door and morning sickness pulled her back in. She had prepared herself for this day and she couldn't get one foot out the door without detouring to the bathroom.

Tears ran from Nikki's eyes as she left the bathroom, hurriedly putting one foot in front of the other to make it out the door. Before her hand could hold on to the knob she was on her way back to the bathroom and her head was back into the toilet bowl. Nikki wasn't going to accept defeat; she had to take her finals. Once again she stood on her feet and washed her mouth at the sink. "You are not going to stop me!" she yelled at her stomach. "I have to do this to prepare a good future for us. Do you hear me! I have to take my test." She was already scolding her unborn child. "You weren't a part of my plan but you are now. Regardless of the fact that your father wants you dead Mommy loves you." She cried, "Please help Mommy get out the door. Please let me do this for us." Nikki made it as far as the living room and decided to sit for a while. Nausea brought her ass to the couch.

The long hand of the clock was on five and the short was on nine. The test was scheduled to begin at 9:30 a.m. and there was no way she could make it in five minutes.

"No! No," she screamed like a wounded animal. Her textbook was on the coffee table and Nikki took out her frustration, ripping it to pieces like a shredder.

"I hate you! I hate you." She threw the vase that resided on the coffee table as a centerpiece into a picture that hung on the hall. The vase and the glass frame met with each other and shattered into pieces. The picture was of her and Mark during happier times. "I wasn't supposed to be like this!" She picked herself up. "How could you leave me when I needed you the most?"

All her planning and studying was in vain. She had derailed her own dreams of becoming a heart surgeon. She sobbed, looking at herself in the mirror, feeling disappointed and betrayed.

Nikki locked herself inside the house for days. She wasn't accepting phone calls or even answering her doorbell.

A few days had passed and Mark went by the house to apologize but when he tried to open the door, the chain restricted his entry. All his calls got sent to voicemail. It'd been almost a week since he last saw her. He dialed the number again and like always he left a message. "I'm sorry for what I said about the baby and I'm concerned about you. Call me. I'm sorry."

The phone made several beeps, awaking Nikki from her slumber. She got out of bed and her feet entered her awaiting bed slippers. You could tell that her appearance was the least of her worries. Nikki hadn't eaten a good meal in days she was constantly munching on crackers because that was the only thing the baby seemed to accept. She lazily walked to the bathroom and heavily covered her toothbrush with Crest whitening toothpaste. She took a long look in the mirror and fear took over the once-glowing look that was in her eyes. She was worried, scared, vulnerable, and pregnant. *Was I really blinded by love?*

Chapter 21

Beep. Beep. Nikki's phone indicated that she had a text message. Nikki tried to locate her cell phone with one hand feeling around on the bed. She took the phone back into hiding under the cover. Realizing the text was from Mark, Nikki's head popped up from under the sheet. I'll be back from out of town in a week. I'm going to do the right thing.

That was all Nikki needed to hear. She listened to all his messages and was starting to believe that he was sorry for the way he handled the situation.

"He's going to do the right thing. He's going to propose." She found the strength to get out of bed. "I have a wedding to plan." She was overjoyed. "He just needed some time to think, that's all. He loves me. Mark loves me," she assured herself. "He was just caught off-guard by the fact that I was pregnant. In all honesty I wasn't ready for a child either."

One week was all the time she needed to get everything set up for her wedding. She was going to wait for an engagement ring. When Mark returned he wouldn't have to ask, "Will you marry me?" But instead he would say, "I do."

She was going to need some extra help. Only a few people knew about her relationship with Mark because Mark wanted it that way. Nikki ran through her phone book and stopped at Tina's name. "Should I call her for help?"

Nikki procrastinated. But her best friend, Genie, was all the way in Massachusetts. Tina was the closest person who could be there in no time. Nikki hit the send button and put the phone on speaker because her hands were busy brushing her tangled hair, which she hadn't combed through in days. "Girl, I need your help. How soon can you get here?" Nikki frowned her face as the comb raked through the knotted hair.

"What is the urgency?" Tina questioned.

Nikki pick up the phone and spoke directly into it. "I have a big project to do and I need your help. So how soon can you get here?"

"In ten minutes."

Nikki finally got the knots out of her hair and stripped her clothes off. Her body's frame was smaller than usual. You can tell she lost a few pounds from not being able to eat anything. She entered the shower and the water spewed from the showerhead. She jumped back when the hot water hit her body. She sidestepped, reaching for the gauge, and adjusted the temperature. She turned her backside to the water and tilted her head back. The warm water soaked through her hair, quickly reaching her scalp. The water trickled down her back, running smoothly over her round chocolate ass. She shampooed her hair and the suds slowly slid down her back, caressing her ass, then down to her feet. The aroma from the green-apple shampoo filled the air. Her fingers massaged her scalp, relaxing and de-stressing her body. Nikki rinsed the suds from her hair and reached for her body wash. She lathered her body, feeling like a renewed woman.

The doorbell chimed and she quickly ended her shower. She half opened the door with her towel covering her nakedness.

Tina stood with her hands on her hips. "Are you going to let me in or not?" Nikki walked away from the door with Tina following her. "I need details. What's the big project?" Tina followed her to the bedroom. Nikki released the towel from her head and her wet hair cascaded down her back. "All of a sudden you are mute."

Nikki took a deep breath and exhaled. "I need your help to plan my wedding within a week." The scream Tina let out made Nikki cover her ears.

"Let me see the ring, girl." She took Nikki by the hand but didn't see the diamond. "Where is it?"

Nikki pulled her hand away. "There's none." She walked to her closet.

"What?" Tina questioned.

"He didn't actually propose but—"

"But he wants to skip the engagement and get married," Tina finished her sentence.

"Not really."

"What exactly are you saying, Nikki?" Tina asked, afraid to hear the answer.

"I just need your help to plan a surprise wedding that's all."

"No, Nikki. You can't be serious," Tina said, shaking her head, already knowing it was a bad idea.

"If you won't help me then I suggest you leave." Nikki pulled on pink Victoria's Secret sweatpants with the words LOVE PINK written across her butt.

"Nikki, if that man wanted to get married he would have proposed to you."

"It's either you're with me or against me. So which is it?" Nikki stared at her for the answer.

After a brief moment of silence Tina reluctantly gave her answer. "I have your back. I'll catch you when you fall."

"I thought so." Nikki walked out of the bedroom and went to the bathroom. She retrieved her blow dryer from under the sink.

"Can I just ask you one question?" Tina asked.

"What is it, Tina?" She plugged the dryer in.

"What's the rush, Nikki?"

Nikki turned the dryer on, blocking out anything else Tina had to say.

"I honestly thought you wanted me to come over here and help you with a presentation for a job. Because I know you had to have aced your finals. I had no idea I was going to plan a wedding!" Tina yelled over the sound from the dryer. Nikki turned the dryer off and hovered over the sink with tear escaping from her eyes.

"I'm sorry if I hurt your feelings," Tina consoled her. Nikki cried, pounding her fist on the sink. "What's wrong, Nikki? Please talk to me."

"I'm so stupid. I'm so stupid. I'm smarter than this. How could I be such a fool?"

Tina was clueless as to what Nikki was rambling about. "First it was a surprise wedding. Now you're crying, cursing yourself. Are you okay? Because now you are scaring me."

Nikki wiped her eyes and looked up at herself in the mirror. "I derailed my own dreams," Nikki cried out.

Tina brushed a few loose strands of hair from Nikki's face. "What are you taking about, Nikki? You're not making any sense."

"I didn't get to take my finals. I'm pregnant." Tina paused and took a step back. Nikki walked out of the bathroom. "All that I've been preparing for is out the window."

"This is just a minor setback." Tina ran after her, stopping in front of her. Tina wrapped her arms around her. "It's going to be okay. I'm here for you."

"And so is Mark. He loves me, Tina. We are going to be a family. That's why you have to help me plan this wedding."

Tina looked at Nikki and knew she wasn't thinking straight. She was bouncing from one subject to the next trying to cover up her pain and disappointments. "I need to have everything ready for him to marry me when he gets back." Nikki wasn't her normal self and Tina was worried but she decided to go along with Nikki's wedding plans. Nikki was hurting and if this was what would make her happy Tina was going to be there for her.

The days went by fast it was two days before Mark was expected to return. She spoke to Mark a few times but their conversations were short because he was always too busy to talk to her. "I love you, Mark," she said at the end of every conversation, and his reply would be, "I have to go; I'm busy." Nikki was starting to second-guess her decision. With Mark's attitude she was starting to wonder if he was going to be back on the day he said.

Nikki lazily got out of bed but before her feet could hit the ground her guts wanted to come up. Her head was in the toilet bowl more often than she would have liked. "If my morning sickness keeps getting the best of me I won't even make it to my wedding." She gargled with mouthwash and rinsed her mouth. She dragged herself to the kitchen and poured some orange juice.

The doorbell rang and she said, "Who could that be?" She was hoping that it wasn't Mark but was also anticipating his return. She approached the door and her right eye looked through the peephole. Three bridesmaids stood with their hands behind them. *They are trying to hide my presents.* Nikki was gleeful. She opened the door and their hands came forward and sprayed her with streamers.

"How do you feel the day before your wedding?" Her friend, Genie, shouted with joy.

"What if Mark was here? You would ruin everything."

"The wedding is tomorrow and he's still not back. I would be worried if I were you," Lashawn said, spraying more streamers on her head.

"Don't worry, Nikki, he will be back and he will say yes. I mean I do," Genie stated as she helped Nikki take the streamers from her body. "And how is my little niece or nephew doing?" Genie rubbed her belly.

"I still can't keep anything down."

Lashawn sprayed more streamers on her belly. "You need to get dressed. We have a big day planned for you."

Nikki and her bridesmaids spent the day pampering themselves with pedicures, manicures, and a spa treatment, but Nikki kept checking her phone to make sure that she didn't miss any calls from Mark. Genie tried to be optimistic of the whole situation, but Tina had something negative to say every time Nikki turned her back. "Somebody needs to tell her the damn truth." Tina looked at Genie.

"Why are you looking at me?" Genie snapped.

"You are supposedly her best friend." Tina snapped back at her.

"Maybe you are just damn jealous," Genie attacked.

"What the hell are you two arguing about? Nikki wants to plan a surprise wedding without Mark's knowledge that is her damn business!" Lashawn scolded.

"But I just know it's ridiculous." Tina gave her last word.

"Well you don't have to be a part of it then." Genie stated her last words too.

Nikki reentered the room and heard Genie's statement. "Don't have to be a part of what?" Nikki curiously asked.

"Go ahead, Tina, fill her in."

Tina didn't say a word. She remained silent.

***

The next morning Nikki woke up early. Her antici-
pation wouldn't allow her to sleep. She was filled with
anxiety. She lowered her feet to the floor but she felt
something other than her bed slippers and hastily pulled
her feet back. She had forgotten that Tina and Lashawn
had made beds on the floor. They had a long night last
night reminiscing about old times and stuffing their
bodies with calories from popcorn. She stepped over the
two squatters, not wanting to wake them. She wanted to
get a head start in the bathroom before all the bickering
started. She viewed herself in the mirror and took a
deep breath, trying to get rid of the jitters that were now
consuming her nerves.

"Hi, early bird." Tina entered the bathroom and went
straight for the toilet and emptied her bladder. Nikki
grabbed her heart, covering her eyes, as she recovered
from an almost heart attack. "You want me to make you
breakfast?" Tina asked as she flushed the toilet.

"Are you planning on washing your hands?"

"Maybe I should add some flavor to the scrambled
eggs." She wiggled her hands in Nikki's face.

"You are so disgusting."

Tina pushed her out of the way and stuck her hands
under the faucet. "So did he call?" Tina inquired.

"He said he was coming back today and I believe he is,"
she said as she stepped into the shower.

"Say no more!" Tina left the bathroom.

Nikki finished her shower and the aroma of scrambled
eggs and pancakes hit her nostrils. She adorned her robe
and made her way to the kitchen. *I hope this baby will
allow me to have a nice breakfast on my wedding day.*

"Something sure smells good." Lashawn said as she came out of the bedroom, and Genie was right behind her.

"You hungry vultures better go take care of your morning breath before entering the kitchen."

"Good morning Mrs. Gray! ," Lashawn said, walking past her.

"That does sound good. Say it again." Nikki had a wide smile from ear to ear.

"Are you ready for your honeymoon, Mrs. Gray?" Genie asked.

"Hell yes, I am." Nikki and Genie both screamed as they hugged each other.

"What's all this commotion?" Tina asked as she ran from the kitchen with the spatula in her hand and witnessed Genie and Nikki jumping around like two kids at recess.

After breakfast Lashawn did Nikki's hair. She gave her an up do to show off her high cheekbones. Her hair turned out beautiful. Lashawn was a hairdresser, not by trade, but somehow she learned the craft by watching her aunt, who was a professional. Genie was going to wear her hair down so she was next to get her hair flat ironed, while Tina was getting her makeup done. Finally getting some time to herself Nikki seized the moment and went to her bedroom and called Mark.

"Hello," Mark answered in a husky voice.

"Hi, honey! I can't wait to see you."

"I'm actually leaving the airport right now. I'll be there in a few."

Nikki did a little dance.

"I'll talk to you later." Mark was about to dismiss her.

"Mark! Mark! Before you go, I'm going to need you to pick me up from Emmanuel Apostolic Church; the one around the corner from my job."

"Why?"

Nikki cleared her throat and prepared to sell her lie. "I'm attending a fundraiser and by the time you get here it should be wrapping up. So I figure we can go get something to eat and talk after."

"No problem. I have to go."

"I love you, baby."

Nikki opened the bedroom door and the house was filled with excitement. Concerned bridesmaids questioned if they could still fit in their dresses. "Oh my God!" Nikki ran to the kitchen where Tina was getting her makeup done. "He's on his way!"

"And what's the problem?" Tina questioned.

"He can't get to the church before me, the wedding will be ruined."

Tina got up out of the chair and she sat down. "Can you go get dressed and tell Lashawn and Genie to hurry up please?" Nikki's phone beeped, indicating she had a text message. She looked at her phone and the message was from Mark. Her heart started to pound as she anxiously read it.

You're willing to spend the rest of your life with me but I'm so far from perfect. I've been carrying a burden on my shoulders and today I will relieve myself of it.

What does this mean? Am I the burden he speaks of? Is he going to rid me from his life? No, I can't be.

She read the message a second time, skeptical of what Mark was saying. *He's probably going to confess to a lie that he told me, but today is our wedding day. I will just have to forgive him.*

"He loves me and that's all that really matters." She inhaled and exhaled, dismissing her jitters.

It didn't take long to do her makeup because she wanted it simple. But Bryanna, her makeup artist, managed to convince her to try some fake lashes. A light foundation and mascara to pop her eyes was enough for her. The pink lip gloss made her lips full.

"We have to cut this right now. I have to go get dressed." She got up off the chair and hurried to her bedroom, where her bridesmaids were looking themselves over in the mirror. They all looked elegant in their fuchsia strapless dresses that were complemented by silver high-heel pumps. Nikki fanned her face with her hand because she was delighted to see how spectacular they looked.

Seeing them looking so beautiful makes me wish the wedding were happening under different circumstances. Not to mention the text message I kept trying to decipher. I think am suddenly having cold feet.

Nikki all of a sudden looked flustered. But she didn't want to embarrass herself so she proceeded in pretence.

Nikki adorned herself in the perfect wedding dress. It wasn't too fancy; it was simple but elegant. The drapery was done beautifully and hid any sign of her pregnancy. Her stylist zipped the back of her dress and it stopped in the gape of her back.

"This can't be happening."

"Just inhale deeply. It's just a little baby fat."

She took a deep breath and the zipper went up without a hitch. She stepped into her heels then viewed herself in the mirror and her eyes became glassy with tears.

"Oh no you don't!" Bryanna grabbed a piece of tissue from the box and dabbed her eyes. "Save the tears until after you say I do. I will not allow you to ruin your makeup."

"Okay. Okay," Nikki agreed, sniffling.

"Your bridesmaids are waiting to see the blushing bride." Bryanna opened the door and her anxious bridesmaids let out gasps. Nikki looked radiant as her smile stretched from ear to ear.

A horn sounded outside and Genie looked through the peephole and saw the limousine. They hurriedly added their final touches and Bryanna helped Nikki with her veil.

"Wait! Something borrowed, something blue, something old, and something new," Nikki said anxiously.

Three things from the list were checked off but there was nothing blue in sight. Nikki panicked but was reassured when they convinced her that the list was nothing more than an old wives' tale.

"All that nonsense about stepping over a crack will break your mother's back is nonsense. Honestly I think someone came up with that scheme to get more handouts on her wedding day. Something borrowed, old, new my ass." They all laughed at Genie's statement.

The day was perfect, not a cloud in sight. The temperature was just right. Summer was coming to a close so the sun wasn't beaming. Nikki reminisced on her past, present, and her hopes for the future with Mark. She pictured her house in the suburbs with a well-manicured lawn and also a big backyard for her baby to run around in. Thoughts of Keisha ran across her mind.

"Are you ready to go walk down the aisle and finally become Mrs. Shavelle Nicolette Gray?"

"Come on, girl, we have to go," Lashawn said.

Genie picked up the train of Nikki's dress. "Lashawn, get the door," Genie ordered.

"Here comes the bride, here come the bride." Lashawn sang, turning the lock on the door. "Here comes the bri ..." Her mouth remained open when she saw Mark at the door.

"What's going on?" Mark asked.

Lashawn stepped back so Mark could see his blushing bride. It was as if Nikki's feet were glued to the ground.

"Why are you wearing a wedding dress?" Mark stood at the door without taking a step.

"What are you doing here? You were supposed to meet me at the church."

Everyone was frozen in time. All her bridesmaids were speechless. Nikki wanted to run into his arms but her legs wouldn't let her.

"Let me guess. I was supposed to show up at the church to our wedding?" Mark finally came inside and stood in front of her. "Is that right, Nikki?" She took Mark's hands and he released her grip and Nikki knew instantly that it was not good. Inside she was praying that Mark wouldn't embarrass her. But the look on Mark face said it all. There wouldn't be a wedding.

"Have you lost your damn mind?"

"I know you are a little surprised but you can't do this to me," Nikki pleaded.

"You lied to me!" Mark yelled. Nikki held his arm and he pulled away his arm. "Don't touch me!"

"Mark, we have a baby on the way. Please make me your wife."

"You are trying to use this damn baby to trap me! I told you I didn't want this damn child!" He turned to walk away and Nikki grabbed on to him.

"Mark, I love you." She fell to her knees. Genie ran to her. She held on to Genie for support. *Dear God, please don't let him walk out on me. Dear God, please don't let him humiliate me like this.* She squeezed on to Genie's hand. "What do you want me to do?"

Tina looked intently at Mark, pointing her index finger at him. "It is only a cowardly man who breaks the heart of a woman and guards his own. But it's also selfish of a woman to live in denial being ignorant to the truth." She finished her speech, looking down at Nikki.

Mark walked out the door and Nikki ran after him. "Mark, I love you. We can be a family. Let me be your wife."

"We can't get married, not now, not ever!"

"What about the text you sent me? You said you wanted to make thing right."

"I shouldn't have let this situation between us go so far. It wasn't my intention to hurt you but I allowed myself to get caught up in this nonsense."

"Nonsense!" Nikki was confused.

The expression on Mark's face said it all. This wasn't the man she knew; this man who stood before her was a stranger. There was no love in his eyes or warmth in his voice. He couldn't look her in the eye because he knew what he was about to say would hurt her.

"Mark, please, you can't do this to us. What's going on? I know you, Mark. Please tell me what wrong," Nikki pleaded with him.

"You don't know me! If you did you would know my damn name isn't Mark!"

You could hear the gasps from the girls. Nikki couldn't believe what she was hearing. "What did you say?"

"The truth is, I don't work for a cable company, and—"

"What?" Nikki questioned. "That day you came here to fix the cable . . . you were wearing . . . and you were driving . . ." Nikki sentences were incomplete.

"Allan at the cable company is a friend and he was in on it. That day when you went looking for me at my so-called job . . . That's why they didn't know who I was."

"Okay, you lied about your job. We can still get married." Nikki walked closer to him. "The pastor is at the church is waiting for us."

"I'm already married!"

Chapter 22

Keisha sat at the Jamaican restaurant, enjoying some oxtail and rice, waiting for Bling to join her. He was at the studio working on a collaboration with a few artists including Hype. She was facing the door when she saw Mark enter looking miserable and she called him over. Mark rushed over to her and from a closer look she could tell his blood was boiling.

"We have to talk!" Mark's voice was loud enough for all heads to turn.

"Are you Mark, or is it Damien? Which is it today? I think I'll call you Mark. Is there trouble in paradise?"

"I'm done with this shit! You win."

Her phone was on the table and it was now ringing and it was Bling calling. "Hold that thought." A big smile appeared. "Hello!" she answered, but Bling didn't respond. "Let me guess, you just called to hear my voice." The call ended. "What the hell was that about? He probably butt dialed me." She could barely finish her sentence when Mark grabbed the phone out of her hand.

"What the fuck is your problem?" She grabbed her phone back.

"It's done. It's over!"

The phone started to ring and it was Bling calling back. Mark was trying talk to her but she was self-consumed at the moment. "If this is your butt calling me again I have a few thinks to say. I miss your touch. I miss your lips all over my body."

Mark walked out of the restaurant frustrated and upset.

"I need you, baby. Say something. Tell me how much you miss me too." She spoke in a seductive tone.

"You fucking bitch!" Hype yelled in her ear.

Instantly her whole body felt paralyzed. This was one controversy she couldn't slide her way out of. *Why is he using Bling's phone? Did Bling set me up?* A thousand questions ran through her mind. She remembered entering her name as Your Little Freak in Bling's phone and she knew he had to see it if he in fact was the one who dialed her number. She held the phone to her ear frozen, speechless, thoughtless, and in fear because she knew she would have to pay for her betrayal and her penalty could be death. With the phone still glued to her ear she heard the chaos in the studio.

"I guess we have something in common besides music." Hype had confronted Bling with his gun.

"What the hell is he talking about?" She could hear the panic in Bling's voice. She heard Bling's friend telling him to put the gun down. Everybody was trying to figure out what had Hype so upset that he wanted to take Bling's life.

"How long have you been sleeping with my woman?"

Keisha picked up her pocketbook and left a fifty dollar bill on the table. She was making a mad dash out the door when Mark grabbed her arm, causing the phone to fall on the ground.

"I said we need to talk!"

"Get off me!" She pulled away from him. She was on the ground like a crackhead searching for a hit. Luckily her phone was still intact and the commotion in the studio was still going. She ran to her car and reversed out of the parking lot with one hand on the steering wheel and the other held the phone at her ear.

"How long have you been sleeping with Keisha?" Bling neither denied nor confirmed the allegation. "I should end your life right now."

Keisha tried pleading with him, not knowing if they could hear her. "Hype, I'm sorry that you find out this way. But please don't do anything you might regret. I know that I was wrong. I can't undo what I've done but two wrongs don't make a right."

Her pleading fell on deaf ears because the commotion got even louder. "Put the gun down, Hype! Don't do this, man!" She could hear them pleading with him.

"Pull the trigger or I'm giving you one second to get the gun out my face." She finally heard Bling's voice but he wasn't saying what she wanted to hear.

"I'll spare your life so you can live to see me fucking your wife because she is just a cheap whore wearing expensive clothes."

Keisha heard the commotion get louder. Bling didn't take the statement lightly. She knew they were fighting. She heard the guys trying to restrain them. She heard the gun fire and the room was in complete silence as the bullet penetrated someone's body.

"Nooo. Oh my God, no." Keisha stepped on the brake in the middle of the road, causing a chain reaction.

The microphone fell and hit the floor, making a loud sound that broke the silence. She knew something was wrong, terribly wrong. Someone has been shot. Thinking it was Bling she called out his name repetitively. "Bling, Bling! Say something!" Tears ran out of her eyes because she knew she was also at fault for someone's senseless death. "He's going to come looking for me. I have to leave this place."

It was like a parade of honking horns trying to get Keisha to get out of the road. She finally drove off when the car behind her intentionally bumped into her rear, not hard enough to leave a dent but enough to bring her back to reality. She made it home safe but she was weak in her knees. She parked her car and as fast as her legs could move she hurried to the door. She was going to run inside and pack as many clothes as she could fit in her suitcase. Her brain wasn't sending the signals to her hands or fingers because she was fumbling with her keys. She couldn't open the door and she was in tears.

"I said we need to talk!" She heard Mark's voice yelling from the sidewalk.

Keisha ignored him. She finally got the key in the keyhole but before she could get inside Mark ran up the steps and grabbed her by her neck.

"You think you run shit don't you?"

"Are you all right, young lady?" an elderly man stopped to ask.

Mark released Keisha and turned to address the man. "If you want to live to see another day, I suggest that you mind your damn business."

The old man stood his ground and addressed Keisha again. "Do you want me to call the police?

"I'm fine!" she barked at the old man.

"I'm still calling the police."

Mark went down the steps and Keisha hurried inside and closed the door behind her.

Mark banged on the door. "Open this damn door!"

Keisha ran to her bedroom, taking her Louis Vuitton luggage set from under the bed, and tossed her clothes inside.

"This isn't over. I'll be back." Mark kicked the door.

Keisha didn't have time to organize; she just tossed clothes, shoes, and perfume in the suitcase until it was overflowing. She sat on the top and closed it. She dragged it to the door and looked out to see if Mark was still outside. She saw no sign of him and she dragged the suitcase to her car. She ran back in the house, leaving the door open behind her. She grabbed the duffle bag and stuffed more clothes inside. Keisha zipped the duffle bag and turned to the door and Mark was standing there. "So you were just going to leave town. And expect me to take the heat."

Keisha dropped her bag. "Mark, this isn't what it looks like." Mark walked closer to her and she took a step back. "Hype is coming after me and I have to leave."

"Well, Houston, we have a problem." He walked closer to her.

"Mark, I have to go. Figure out your shit with Nikki."

"Did you know that your friend planned a secret wedding for us? Where did she get that bright idea?"

"Mark, I didn't know anything about it."

"You expect me to believe you?"

"Believe whatever you want. But I have to leave town for a while. I can't worry about your shit right now."

"Shit is about to hit the fan and you are leaving town."

"Right now my life is in danger. I have to go, so you better handle that mess you created."

"The mess I created? This was your big plan to destroy her."

"You were supposed to take her to the movies and distract her from her studying that's all. Don't come here blaming me. You took it as far as it went."

"But I did it for you!"

"So are you expecting a pat on your back?"

"I did everything you asked me to do but you are never going to forgive me. You lied to me. You were never going to take me back. You are a selfish bitch!" Mark punched the wall with his fist.

"I wasn't selfish when I helped you keep your damn restaurant. That was the deal, don't you remember?"

"Why did you sleep with me at the restaurant?"

"Just to torture you so you can see what you missed out on."

"You are still my wife!"

"Stop calling me your damn wife. We never got divorced because it wasn't a priority for me at the time and I forgot about it just like I forgot about you; until you pop up in my life like a damn wounded dog, begging me to help save your damn restaurant because your woman left you broke. I felt sorry for you, Mark, and I helped you with the cash. But I had to knock Nikki off her high horse and you fell into place. Our relationship ended years ago. And get this through your thick skull: I will never be your woman again. I'm not a naïve teenager anymore. I have men eating out of the palm of my hand."

"You are a damn whore!" he shouted from his gut.

"Fuck you, Mark! Oops, I mean Damien!"

"I did everything you asked me to do. I messed up Nikki's life to make you happy. Keisha, we could be happy again."

"There will be no us. You damn loser." Her words hit him where it hurt. His hands were around her neck. Keisha was trying to loosen his grip but he wanted to kill her. But he suddenly released his grip and she fell to the floor, gasping for air.

"By the way Nikki is a better lay than you any day." He walked out of the room.

"I hate you!" She ran after him but the two of them stopped suddenly when they saw Nikki.

"Why?" Nikki roared like a lion.

They were both speechless. If they could have disappeared they would have.

Nikki stood at the door with her phone in her hand. "You can hang up your phone now. Your phone called me and I answered, thinking you were coming back. Ha-ha. What a joke."

Mark took his phone out of his pocket, and in fact he did call her.

"I heard everything." She was still wearing her wedding dress; it was now soiled from her collapsing outside after hearing Mark's confession. Her makeup was ruined from crying. "I should have known. That day when I came home and you gave me that excuse about you spilling the wine. The day when I came home and you were in my damn house. Oh my God! No wonder you were so upset and barged into my bedroom that night when you found out that he was making love to me. I was so stupid."

"That you are. I told you that you would regret choosing him over me. You got what you deserve," Keisha said, laughing.

"I'm sorry. I didn't mean—" Mark said with his head down.

"Shut your damn mouth!" Nikki slapped him hard before he could say another word.

"You need to give yourself some credit. You reeled him in all by yourself." Keisha was laughing her wicked laugh again.

"You psycho bitch!" Nikki ran toward Keisha like a line back on a football field playing defense. Mark separated them but that was the wrong thing for him to do. "Don't you ever touch me again," Nikki yelled at Mark. "What about the baby?"

"Pregnant!" Keisha repeated, stunned at the news. "Even better than I had planned."

Nikki wanted to rip her apart but she had to think about her unborn child. Her baby meant more to her than kicking Keisha's ass.

"I knew you were a whore hiding behind your books."

"You are a shameless bitch!" Nikki yelled.

"You are still on your high horse even though you're pregnant with a married man's child?"

"You're a bitch with no self-esteem who has to break down your own friend to make yourself feel good. Both of you deserve each other."

"Friend!" Keisha laughed. "You were never my friend. I just let you stay here because I felt sorry for you. I gave you my clothes that were out off season that I didn't want anymore. You were a charity case after your mother died."

"What did I ever do to you for you to want to hurt me like this?"

"It's a simple fact that you fail to remember. No one outshines me! So your college stunt is now null and void."

"You are screwed up in the head. You need to see a psychiatrist. I feel sorry for you."

"Listen to that speech." Keisha clapped. "You deserve an award. Did you write about my life for your final exam?"

Nikki wanted to claw her eyes out. She was the reason for all this. She had messed up her life for her own selfish pleasure.

"What about my baby?" Mark questioned.

Nikki slapped his face in the same spot again and Mark rubbed his cheek clenching his jaw. "You are a sorry excuse for a man. My child will never know you as a father."

Nikki stormed out the door and shots rang out like she was in the middle of a war zone. Nikki's lifeless body descended the steps. Hype was shooting like a madman. Her body lay lifeless on the ground. Her white dress had turn to red. Hype sped off when he realized that he shot the wrong person. Mark rushed to Nikki, checking her pulse, and Nikki was barely breathing.

"Keisha, call 911, call 911!"

Keisha rushed out of the house and tossed her suitcase and duffle bag in the trunk of the car without acknowledging that Nikki had been shot. She drove away.

"How can you be so heartless? She's dying!" Mark called out to her as he held Nikki in his arms.

Chapter 23

The door to Patrick's office was ajar when Keisha got there. She almost pushed the door open but stopped herself when she heard Hype's voice. Her heart started to pound like a drum and she wished she could silence it. She slowly stepped back from the door and eavesdropped on the conversation. Hype was trying to convince Patrick to help him to leave the country but Patrick was apprehensive about getting involved.

"I can't get involve with this mess; besides, this could be bad for business."

"All I need is some money to pay these guys back and leave the country for a while until things cool down."

Hype wasn't telling Patrick the reason he wanted to leave. Keisha was hoping that Patrick would give him the money and send him on his way. She was starting to sweat profusely; even her palm was sweaty. *Give it to him, Uncle, please.* She tried to telepathically send a message to her uncle.

Patrick went in his pocket and took out his wallet. "Here is five hundred dollars. That should buy your plane ticket."

"Five hundred dollars is not going to cut it."

"Not going to cut it? I shouldn't be helping you but I'm willing to give you this money. Take it and leave my office." Patrick was starting to get irate because of Hype's presumptuous attitude. He walked away from him to sit in his chair and Hype followed him.

200 Janice Burkett

"I said five hundred is not going to cut it, so go in your secret stash and give me more money."

Patrick lit a cigar and puffed it a few times with his head tilted back. Hype was now pissed off that Patrick wasn't heeding his request. Hype took out his gun and pointed the gun at Patrick. His cigar fell out of his mouth into his lap. He quickly jumped to his feet, trying to avoid his manhood getting scorched.

"You have five minutes to give me my money."

"I just signed you to my label. I was willing to invest money into your career and now you want to kill me?"

"I don't have to if you do as I say. I need five thousand dollars and you will live to tell the story."

"Get the hell out of my office. I have no money to give to you."

Wrong move, Uncle, just give it to him. Keisha wanted to rush in and defuse the situation but she knew it would only get worse; besides, she was the reason for this mess.

Hype hit Patrick in his face with the gun and his nose started to bleed. Patrick held his nose, looking at the blood in disbelief.

"Now do you take me seriously?"

Patrick walked over to one of the many Bob Marley paintings on the wall and removed it, revealing a safe. He entered the combination to the safe and opened it and money fell to the floor.

"Jackpot from the look of things. Add another five thousand to that."

"Are you crazy?"

Hype pointed the gun at Patrick's head, letting him know how crazy he could be. Patrick quickly took more money out of the safe and handed it to Hype. He stuffed a Gucci bag that he had hanging from his shoulder. Patrick's nose was still bleeding and it was all over the money, but Hype couldn't care less.

"As a matter of fact I'm going to need the keys to your car." Hype was getting greedy and his demand was getting higher. He saw the money and now he wanted it all.

"You are in no position to make that demand. Who the hell do you think you are? Get the hell out my office!"

"Let me introduce myself. I'm the man who is going to end your life."

He shot Patrick in his head. Keisha wanted to scream but in fear of her life she screamed on the inside. She didn't know what to do. Her brain wasn't functioning. She was in panic mode; she couldn't think, feel, or move. She was in a catatonic state.

Hype walked over to the safe and took out all the money and stuffed it into his bag. He stepped over Patrick on his way out. Keisha was still frozen. She was in shock. Hype turned and went back to Patrick, stooping to his level.

"Rule number one: always give up the money."

Hype was on his way out the office and Keisha hid under the secretary's desk. Hype exited the office and dashed outside. Keisha ran to her uncle, unable to contain her emotion.

"Uncle Patrick! Uncle Patrick! You can't die on me."

Hype saw Keisha's car parked outside and came back inside.

She held her uncle's lifeless body and placed his head into her lap. "Talk to me! You can't die. I need you. I need you! You can't die!"

Keisha felt the cold metal at her temple. She knew it was Hype. She clasped her hands and began to say the Lord's Prayer.

"Your messages have been piling up, Mr. Patrick." The secretary strolled in, unaware of what was taking place. "Ahhh!" She screamed in shock at the sight of Hype holding the gun to Keisha's head and then her eyes locked on to Patrick's dead body on the floor. Keisha didn't open her eyes to Angela's screams. She continued praying, hoping her prayer would be answered.

Boom! The gun went off. "Good night, bitch."

Chapter 24

Three months after . . .

Clunk, clunk. The clunking of her six-inch red high-heel pumps made a beat with each step she took.

"Good morning, Angela." Keisha greeted the secretary with a pleasant smile.

"Good morning, Miss Burkett. I have a few messages for you."

"Thank, Angie. I'll retrieve them later. How is your arm healing?"

"I should be good as new in no time."

Keisha strolled to her office knowing today would be a good day because the seventy-two-degree weather outside was perfect and she was bursting with energy. She was the CEO of her uncle's company and everything was going great. She made a promise to herself that she would carry on her uncle's work. Top Dot Records. was the leading record label in the country, despite various attempts to strong-arm her out of business because she was a woman. Keisha handled business like a pit bull in a skirt, proving that she could run the company like any other, if not better. Her whole attitude toward life had changed ever since the day she witnessed her uncle's death. She ruled with an iron fist but she carried herself like a lady.

The red pumps she wore to work that day had her feeling empowered. She stepped into her office and took a deep breath. She could still smell the smell of cigar along with the lingering scent of his cologne. Keisha plopped herself down in the big black leather reclining chair, assuming the position of Mrs. Boss. She looked up at a portrait of her uncle that hung on the wall directly in front of her. She didn't redecorate or rearrange the office. Everything remained the same. Keisha turned her head in bewilderment, still carrying the guilt of Patrick's death. Keisha often felt his presence and she knew for sure that he was there watching over her.

The phone on her desk beeped and Angela's voice came through. "Miss. Burkett, Blaze is here to see you."

"Send him in, Angela." Keisha walked to the file cabinet and retrieved a manila folder. There was a knock on her door even though it was open. Keisha looked up from the file in her hand and signaled him inside.

"I'm glad you could make it." She greeted him with a firm handshake. "Have a seat."

The man's eyes were red from smoking too much weed. Even his cologne was overpowered by the aroma of the weed. Keisha sat in the black leather chair that had her feeling empowered and placed a contract in front of him.

"All that we previously discussed is right there in writing. No changes have been made. My word is concrete."

The man took a quick glance at the contract then looked back at her with his half-closed eyes. "I respect your honesty; that's why I'm riding on your team." The man nodded his head while he spoke and rubbed his hands together. They sounded rough and dry. She wanted to offer him some lotion but figured that would be rude.

"Well since you agree with the terms, you can sign here, here, and here." She pointed out to him the three areas she had marked with an X. Blaze signed on the dotted lines with no hesitations. Keisha got up from her chair and extended her hand with another firm handshake, sealing the deal.

"Congratulations! Welcome to Top Dot Records." Two of her other recently signed artists entered her office but paused at the door when they noticed she was in a meeting. "Come on in, guys. You are just in time. I want to introduce you to your new label mate, Blaze."

The guys greeted each other with their manly hand-shakes while she placed the signed document back into the folder and wrote the word "complete" in bold letters then brought it back to the file cabinet. "I want you three to work on a single together."

"No disrespect, but I thought that spot was for Bling."

Keisha closed the cabinet and turned her body to answer the question. "Bling would rather not be on this single."

"Why? He thinks that he's too much of a big artist to be on a song with us."

"I can't get into it but I'm sure that's not the reason."

The true reason was that Bling was looking to sign with another label to prove to his wife that his affair with Kei-sha was over. Besides, things weren't the same between Bling and Keisha when he found out that she had lied to him from the start. Keisha was willing to give him his space; besides, she had been through so much she wanted some time to heal herself. So much had transpired from that day Johnny had raped her until now. It was like a domino effect. Her life had spiraled out of control.

Keisha phone rang and she viewed the caller ID. "Guys, do you mind stepping outside? I have to take this call."

She followed them to the door and closed the door behind them. "Give me the good news!" She spoke with anxiety in her voice. She hurried to her desk and flipped through her notepad, trying to find a clean sheet of paper. "Go ahead, I'm listening." She wrote the information down in bold letters: C-Pac. Brooklyn, NY.

"Are you sure this information is concrete? Okay. I guess the chase is finally over and he will pay for what he did to my uncle." Her informant had told her that Hype would be performing at a talent competition trying to earn money the only way he could since he was on the run. She hung up the phone then walked over to the Bob Marley painting that hid the safe. 13-9-12. She turned to each number, looking over her shoulder, trying to secure the combination. Keisha retrieved a .45 pistol then returned the painting back to its spot on the wall. Her Gucci pocketbook would shield the weapon from wondering eyes as she exited.

Keisha blew a kiss to her uncle as she exited the office. She walked past the secretary's desk, clutching her pocketbook tight. She wasn't going to inform anyone about her mission. She didn't need reinforcement by the police or anyone; this job was something she had to complete by herself.

"Your messages are piling up," Angela shouted.

"Cancel all my appointments and meetings for today. I don't know when I'll be back," she shouted back as she dashed outside to her car.

Her candy apple Benz answered her when she pressed the button for it to open. She had traded in the one Mr. Money had bought her for this one. She sped off down the street, not caring if a cop was in sight. The thought of finally putting an end to Hype's life was all she cared about. Her destination was to find a beauty supply store and purchase the perfect wig for her disguise because she was going to need one for her new adventure. She also stopped at a CVS pharmacy to pick up a few over-the-counter pills that she would need to make a concoction. Her informant had told her where to find Hype and tonight she would avenge her uncle's death.

***

It was nine p.m. when Keisha exited the Jackie Robinson Parkway onto Pennsylvania Avenue. The traffic came to a halt and she was pissed. It was a small fender bender and instead of pulling to the side the idiots blocked both lanes. When Keisha finally got up close to the scene she put her window down. "Pull over to the side! You dumb ass. The police will tell your dumb ass to pull to the side anyway." She was in a haste trying to get to the club.

She finally turned onto East Forty-eighth and Farragut onto the bumpy, unpaved road leading to the club. When she entered C-Pac the majority of the people were seated, but a few were standing against the wall and at the bar. She scoped out the room trying to find Hype. But her eyes didn't lock on to him.

The host came on stage with a voice bigger than his body and introduced himself as Noah. He was quite amusing as he entertained the crowd, trying to hype them up for the first performer. Keisha cracked a smile because even though she was there with murder on her mind, Noah's antics mixed with his Jamaican accent were really amusing.

The first act came on stage and he started out with a bang but it went sour when he tried to hit a high note that he couldn't carry off. A few boos echoed in the room and the host ran on the stage and took the mike from him. *I need a drink if I'm going to be here listening to this mess.*

Keisha made her way to the bar, tugging on her tight-fitted black dress that was riding up as she walked. The big Gucci shades she wore to hide her eyes were making it hard for her to really see clearly. Her long blond wig cut with a bang made her look mysterious.

"I bring to you Hypnotic!" the host declared and the crowd cheered. Keisha was ordering a tequila shot and didn't bother to look until she heard the voice. Her head turned so fast she could've gotten whiplash. Her hand reached into her purse and felt the cold steel. The shot glass was at her head. The liquor burned her throat but she took it like a man. She was going to walk right up to the stage and kill him. She walked off like a madwoman.

Patience, Keisha, too many witnesses. She heard her uncle's voice speak to her. She slowed her pace and calmed her anxiety. She took a glance over her shades to view the room and try to see if anybody was reading her mind, knowing she was there to commit murder. All eyes were on Hype because there was no denying his talent. He had switched his style from rap to R&B and his voice would put Trey Songz to shame. His voice almost made Keisha forget the reason she was there. Hype turned his head, facing her direction, and she turned herself away from his stare.

Hype got to the peak of his song, hitting the notes on point, and the crowd went wild. Hearing his voice angered Keisha even more. Listening to these females scream his name made her blood boil. She took each agonizing step back to the bar. "You have to wait for the right moment, Keisha," she advised herself.

Hype finished his song on a high note, and as he made his way off stage a few ditsy females ran to get up close and personal with him. He was making his way to the bar and Keisha swirled the stool, turning her back to him. "Which one of you ladies wants to buy me a drink?"

"I will!" the two women said in unison.

"I'll let both of you buy me a drink then."

Hype was standing right next to Keisha. She swallowed hard. She could smell his cologne and recognized the smell. It was Bleu by Chanel. He ordered a Red Bull and rum, which was a dangerous combination. Keisha wished he would drop dead.

"Why don't you two ladies go enjoy the rest of the show so I can decide who is coming home with me tonight."

The two ladies both kissed his cheek and walked off.

"Can I buy you a drink? I see your glass is empty," he said to Keisha.

His offer was ignored. Keisha wanted to kill him right there and then but there were too many witnesses. He lengthened his hand for a handshake and that too was ignored.

"I guess you don't talk to strangers, but my name is Hy . . ." He cleared his throat and took a drink, realizing that he almost gave himself away. "I mean Hypnotic."

Keisha was getting anxious. She wanted to end his life. Hearing him speak made her furious knowing her uncle no longer had that right. She slowly put her hand in her pocketbook, holding the gun. She couldn't contain her anger; she was going to do it. She had to do it. She was coming up with her hand to blow his brains out but just then an acquaintance of Hype's came by the bar and distracted his attention from Keisha. Keisha took it as her cue to step outside and shake off the anxiety.

She hurried to the door almost breaking her ankle in her heels. She paced back and forth, taking deep breaths to calm down. Her breathing was heavy. *Get a hold of yourself. You have a job to do and you have to do it right.* "Uncle, I can't stand knowing he's still breathing and you are dead. He doesn't deserve to live!"

The door opened and a gentleman came outside. "Hey, pretty lady." Keisha took a deep breath and composed herself. She went back inside, ignoring the man.

Keisha made her way to the opposite end of the bar. Hype sneaked up behind her and spoke in her ears, causing her to jump. "I'm glad you came back."

Feeling his breath on her body made her skin crawl. He was coming on too strong and she had to put a stop to it before her cover was blown. *I have to put the sleeping pills in his drink. I have to order him a drink.* Keisha was hesitant to speak out of fear that he would recognize her voice, but she had to make a move or else her plan would fail.

"You luk like yuh need another drink." She summoned the strength to speak and disguised her voice with her Jamaican accent.

Hype looked at his glass, which was almost empty. "Can't say I don't," he agreed with her.

Keisha signaled for the waitress to give him another round. She secretly hoped that the combination of Red Bull and rum would kill him and his blood wouldn't be on her hands.

"You look familiar. Similar to someone I once knew."

Keisha's heart pounded hard in her chest, fearful that her cover had been blown.

He shook his head, dismissing the thought. "But you couldn't be. You are way sexier than her."

Keisha exhaled. "Whatever he's drinking keep dem coming."

"I'm starting to think that you want to get me drunk."

Noah stepped on stage, commanding everyone's attention. "It's time to announce the winners, not the losers." He announced third place, the second-place winner, then Hype's name was called in first place and the crowd cheered.

He left his drink at the bar and Keisha took the opportunity to put in the sleeping pills that she had crushed to powder. Keisha hurriedly took a jar out of her purse and poured it into his drink, since all eyes were on Hype, including the bartender's. She couldn't get the shakiness away. She was nervous thinking someone might see her. She was praying that the powder would dissolve faster. The female admirer who was competing for his attention earlier took him by the hand, pulling him in the opposite direction, and Keisha breathed a sigh of relief. When it was fully dissolved she took it upon herself to walk over to him with the drink. "Yuh left yuh drink a di bar and I don't want mi money going to waste."

Hype took the drink and finished it one shot, thinking he was the man.

"I'm heading home but you seem like you have a story to tell. I'm interested to hear it if you care to join me," Keisha said with regret. But that was the only way to carry out her plan without any witnesses. Besides, it was only a matter of time before the pills would set in.

"I'd gladly accept, but where is home?"

"I'm staying at a hotel nuh far from here."

"Oh, so you're not from around here?"

"Yuh coming or not?" she asked as she headed for the door.

Hype wanted to take his car but Keisha signaled for him to join her in her car. If everything went as planned she would be heading back to Connecticut before the night ended.

She pulled up outside the Marriot and the valet approached to park her car. She handed her key over, then scooted out of the car holding her pocketbook tight.

"Are you checking in?" the employee at the desk asked.

Oh shit. I totally forgot to check in before I went to find Hype. If I check in he's going to know my name.

"Ma'am! Are you checking in?"

Hype's phone started to ring and he answered it.

"Phew." Keisha exhaled as Hype walked away, engaged in his conversation. She hurriedly gave her name and information. She stared at Hype with his back turned to her. How she wished she could just pierce his head with a bullet.

"Here you go, Miss. Burkett." The man handed her the credit card. She turned her head quickly as if she wanted to tell him to shut up. "Room 301 will be your room for the night."

She hurriedly took the key card. Hype walked back to her with his conversation on high. Keisha walked off to the elevator and slid the key card. The door opened promptly.

Hype stepped inside, still on his phone. "You know me, player, I get mine," he said aloud to whoever it was he was speaking to. "I got a diamond tonight. She even looks like a keeper. But I'll fill you in later." He reached out and touched Keisha and her skin crawled.

The door slowly closed and she pressed the number three. Keisha held on to her pocketbook with a firm grip, hoping that Hype didn't get too close to her for her to kill him in the elevator. Her eyes studied the numbers from one to twelve representing each floor. The elevator started to move and her stomach felt like she was on a roller coaster. The number two button lit up and her stomach was in a knot. She didn't know what her next move would be when she got to her room.

"What brought you to town?" Hype asked.

Keisha's eyes were still focused on the numbers. She didn't want to look at him. She hated every fiber of his being. "Mi here on business fe eliminate a problem dat should've been taking care of a long time ago."

"You sound lethal. You're not carrying a weapon are you?" Hype joked.

Keisha gave him a sadistic smile. *If you only know how badly I want to blow your fucking head off.* Keisha tightened her grip on her pocketbook.

"It seems like you have a story to tell. I'm more than willing to listen." He got closer to her but the door opened and Keisha led the way.

"Tell mi 'bout your life as a struggling artist; dat will be more interesting." Keisha was a step ahead, not wanting to walk at the same pace. She paused at room 301 and slid the key card. A green light flashed, giving her the okay to open the door.

The AC was on high and the cold air gave her chills when she entered. Hype grabbed her from behind and Keisha had a panic attack. "Get off me!"

Hype backed up as she ran to the far end of the room. "You can't bring a man to a hotel and not expect him to touch you."

"Yuh tink mi looking for a one-night stand. Me just here pon business fe right a wrong."

"You can right your wrong after you satisfy this man." He was walking over to her, unbuttoning his shirt. "Take your glasses off. I would love to look into your eyes. You're like a mystery that I'm trying to solve." He took his shirt off and lay on the bed. "Come to papa!"

Keisha darted to the bathroom, closing the door behind her. She took her glasses off and splashed her face with water. Hype was banging the door like he wanted to break it down.

"Open the door, baby! I won't bite. I'll be gentle I promise."

Keisha took the gun out of her pocketbook and aimed at the door.

"Don't let me wait too long."

She could hear him walking away from the door. Keisha exhaled, looking at herself in the mirror. She was raging with anger. She didn't want to spend another minute in the room with him. She was going to kill him and the time was now. Keisha unlocked the door and turned the knob, opening the door. *It's better to wait until the sleeping pills set in. I don't want anything to go wrong.* She placed the gun back into her pocketbook and put her glasses back on her face. When she emerged from the bathroom Hype was lying on the bed in his boxers, licking his lips.

"It took you long enough," Hype said as he got up off the bed.

"Wha di hell yuh expecting. Mi look like a whore to yuh?"

"Take off your clothes and show me what you got under that dress."

"Do you think I'm going to sleep with you? Don't get it twisted."

Hype got out off the bed and started to get dressed. He was furious at Keisha. "Why the hell would you pick me up in a bar and invite me to your room if you didn't want to sleep with me? Do you know how many women at the club would've loved to take me home?"

"Why isn't the poison working?" she said through gritted teeth. She didn't want to use the gun if she didn't have to. If the pills would just work she could call the police to come and get him.

"What did you say?"

"I said, 'what position wud you like?'" She tried to cover up what she had originally said.

"You are a character. Now you changed your mind."

"I need yuh company," Keisha lied.

"Then prove it."

She had to convince him to stay because she knew the pills should set in very soon and she wanted him to pass out in her presence. "Is dis what yuh want?" She dropped the straps off her shoulders.

"It's all I want and more." He walked toward her.

She didn't want him to touch her. The repulsive thought made her squirm. She could tell he was starting to feel the effect of the pills. His eyes were half closed and his speech was slurred. "I'm going to . . . give it to you good."

"Come and get it," she taunted, knowing damn well that she didn't want his hands touching her.

Hype took another step and fell to the floor. She looked to the sky. "Finally!" Keisha took her glasses off. She felt his pulse and he was still alive. She took the gun out of her pocketbook and pointed it at his head and her hand started to shake. "I can do this. I can do this. I can kill this motherfucker!" She kicked him hard.

"Mmhh." Hype moaned.

She kicked him again. "This is for my uncle." Tears ran down her face. She wiped her eyes and placed both hands on the gun. She couldn't pull the trigger. She kicked him again and again. "I hate you!" She was shaking uncontrollably. "I can't do it, Uncle! I can't." She saw her reflection in the mirror that overlooked the bed. Keisha hit the mirror with the gun, breaking it. She was disgusted with herself. She walked over to the phone and dialed 911. Keisha could barely get her words out. "I'm . . ." She sobbed uncontrollably.

"Calm down. I can't hear you. What's your location?" the 911 operator asked.

Keisha managed to control her sniffles. "The Marriott . . . Hotel." She could hear the 911 dispatcher typing her answer. "Room 301."

Hype woke up and limped toward her. She was unaware because her crying blocked out any sound.

"The man you're looking for, Jerome Campbell aka Hype, is here. Please hurry." Keisha felt a presence behind her and turned to look. She screamed in disbelief and dropped the phone.

"Ma'am. Ma'am. Are you okay?"

Hype grabbed her by her neck and took the gun from her. "Look at those eyes. So it's really you. I must say you did fool me with that Jamaican accent. But you should have killed me when you had the chance." He squeezed her throat. She fought frantically to get away. Her eyes rolled back in the back of her head and he released her from his grip. Keisha fell to her knees, gasping for air. "You are just a bitch trying to do a man's job. Let me guess, you wanted to take my life like I took your uncle's!

He would be so disappointed in you." He walked away from her, laughing.

She took a piece of the broken glass off the floor and ran toward him. Before he could stop her it was in his chest.

"You bitch!" He butted her with the gun and she fell to the floor. Her hand was bleeding because the glass had cut her. "I treated you like a lady and you played me like a fool." He braced his back against the wall and pulled the piece of glass from his chest. "Ahhh!" Blood squirted all over the room. He took a pillowcase and pressed it on his chest.

"Do you think I wanted to kill your uncle?" He was rummaging through the drawer to find tape to cover his wound. "All he had to do was give me the fucking money. I didn't mean to kill Outrage. I accidentally shot him instead of Bling. I didn't want to shoot your friend Nikki. Those bullets were for you. The one time I decided to trust a woman you fucked with my head."

He took the belt off his pants and wrapped it around his chest, holding the pillowcase in place. He kept on rambling as he got dressed. "I was supposed to be a star. I was supposed to go on tour but instead I'm on the run. Get up! Get the fuck up!" He pulled her by her hair and the wig came off. "What a fucking joke. I can't believe you fooled me."

The hit made Keisha dizzy. Everything was a blur. Even Hype's words sounded like a bad phone connection. "Listen carefully. We are going to walk out of here like we are in love; you are going to stay close to me as if we are conjoining twins. The few minutes it will take us to get outside, you're going to be the happiest you have ever been."

Chapter 25

The elevator door opened to the lobby and Hype held her close. He scoped the lobby swiftly, making sure there was no police. A woman was at the counter checking in. the automatic door open permitting a lesbian couple who couldn't keep their hands off each other entry to the lobby. A man with his briefcase came toward them, talking on his cell phone. Confirming that it was safe to walk out without being noticed, Hype proceeded to the door. The automatic door parted for him to exit but before he could put one foot in front of the other four police cars with their lights rotating pulled up outside.

Hype stepped to the side wrapping both of his arms around Keisha with a tight embrace. The pressure from the hug made him cringe as pain from his wound shot through his body. The police came rushing in the lobby with guns drawn. He planted his lips on Keisha, giving the impression that they were in a mating session.

The last police that entered the lobby lingered, looking in their direction. Keisha made eye contact with the cop, hoping he would see her cry for help. She parted her lips to speak and Hype planted another kiss on her lips. With it being clear that everything was okay the police hurried to the elevator.

"Clear!" a policeman shouted to the other five cops ahead of him. Hype held her arm tight and walked outside. A cab was dropping off a passenger and Hype almost knocked them over in a haste to get in the cab.

"Church Avenue. Brooklyn," he ordered.

"Church Avenue and what?" the cabbie inquired with his thick Indian accent.

"Just drive." The cabbie did as he was told.

He was a little weak because even though the pills weren't strong enough to knock him out they still had some effect on him. He was also losing blood but he was fighting to stay awake. Keisha was still woozy from him knocking her over the head with the gun. The whole ride Hype had the gun jammed into her rib cage just in case she tried to do anything stupid.

Keisha rested her head against the door and drifted off sleeping. *You have to be strong. You can do this. You can get through this, baby girl.* Patrick's voice reassured her. *I don't know how, Uncle. He's going to kill me. You have to tell me how, Uncle. I need you.* She felt a hard tug on her arm like the person wanted to rip it off her body. Her vision was blurry as she slowly opened her eyes.

"That will be $25.50," the cabbie said. Realizing she was at their final destination Keisha sat up quickly to face her demise. Hype took out the envelope with his winnings from last night and gave the cabbie fifty bucks. "I have no change for this." The cabbie turned, looking at him angrily.

"Keep the change." He pulled Keisha by her arm out of the cab and the man thanked Hyped continuously for his generous tip. Keisha lazily placed one foot in front of the next as Hype dragged her to a basement apartment.

Hype banged on the door and the lock hanging from the steel bar made the noise even louder. A dog was barking in the apartment, ready to attack. "Who is it?" a man inquired from inside.

"Just open the damn door," Hype stated in anger.

You could hear the many locks being pulled. When the door was open the foul stench of dog pee and musk rushed to Keisha's nostril, making her hurl. "Who is this with you, man? You know I don't like strangers at my place," the man said, trying to see past Hype. Hype pulled Keisha into clear view. "Women are always welcome." He rubbed his palms together.

"Well, she is yours if you want her." Hype pushed Keisha toward the man and she fell down two flights of stairs into the man's arms. They stumbled backward and Keisha fell, hitting her head hard on the tile floor. The dog barked hysterically.

"Why the fuck did you do that?"

Hype made his way down the steps and the dog growled at him. The pit bull was fierce and it wanted to rip him to shreds but lucky for Hype he was in his cage. The pit bull watched intently as Hype walked past his cage.

"Who the fuck is this chick?" The man got up off the floor, looking back at Keisha.

"That bitch from Top Dot Records." Hype reclined on the sofa.

"Don't tell me that you went after her?" The man limped toward Hype.

"She came searching for me. I had everything all planned out. With the money I got I was going to pay Mikey to—"

"Who the hell is Mikey?" the man interrupted.

"My connection with the boat. He was going to take me to the Bahamas. I would be free. This bitch had to mess shit up." Hype got up and headed for the door. The dog barked at him. "Shut the fuck up before I put two bullets in your fucking head!" It was as if the dog comprehended every word Hype said and he lay quietly in his cage.

"Where are you going, man?"

"I'll be back in an hour. Make sure this bitch doesn't move."

The man shook his head in disapproval. "I don't want any part of this mess."

Hype turned the knob and opened the door, then turned to face his friend. "How about her playing the park of your bitch while I'm gone? I know you haven't had pussy in a while." Hype left with a big smile on his face.

His friend closed the many locks on the door, then picked Keisha up off the floor, taking her to the couch. Keisha was too weak to defend herself. Her brain wasn't sending any signal to her body parts. Inside she was kicking and screaming, putting up a fight, but it was futile. He dropped his boxers and his manhood was already hard. He got down on his knees, kissing her legs. He had a toe fetish. "French-manicured toenails." He sucked her toes until he was satisfied.

Keisha found the strength to lift her head but quickly returned it to the comfort of the couch because the pain intensified in her head. Tears streamed down her face as she lay lifeless to his touches. He raised her dress and her lace red panties turned him on even more. He kissed her lower body all over. Keisha felt disgusted as he removed her underwear. The man smiled at her flesh. She fought with whatever energy she could summon up. He was too strong for her and he overpowered her.

Keisha closed her eyes, hoping to fall asleep and reconnect with her uncle but she couldn't sleep through the ordeal. She wanted him to stop. Keisha's eyes were closed through the whole ordeal. She didn't want to see this animal on top of her. She felt his hands cupping her breasts. She also felt his warm tongue. He was suckling like a newborn. Keisha eyes watered and her tears ran like a stream. He kissed her cheek as if to say thanks. She turned her head quickly to the right and it made the room spin. He removed himself from her wetness and fixed her dress, then pulled up his boxers and went to the kitchen.

Keisha had wanted to get revenge for her uncle's death. Hype was supposed to be terminated. How did it backfire on her? *It wasn't supposed to be like this; it wasn't supposed to be like this!* She sobbed quietly and drifted off into sleep.

"I hate what's happening to you," Patrick said.

A woman stood beside Patrick but she had her back turned so Keisha couldn't recognize her face. "Who is with you, Uncle? And why do I feel like I know her?" Keisha suddenly felt a deep connection with the woman. It was as if she knew who she was. She remembered her father telling her that her mother was sick and in the hospital. Without saying another word she knew instantly that the woman was her mother. "Mommy!" she cried, reaching for her. They embraced each other and they sobbed together. "I'm sorry, Mommy! I'm so sorry." Keisha tried to hold on to her mother, not wanting to let go, but she felt someone shaking her and pulling her away from her mother. Keisha was trying to hold on but she lost her grip. "Mommy, please come back. Please come back."

Keisha awoke from her dream to the smell of eggs and bacon. The man had made breakfast and served her a plate. After what he did to her she didn't want to accept his breakfast but she needed to eat to retain energy if she wanted to avenge her uncle's death. She managed to raise herself up and looked into the eyes of her rapist and made a vow to herself. *Revenge will be mine.*

Chapter 26

Later in the night Hype returned and took Keisha to another location. It was a secluded area that accommodated a few abandoned houses. Keisha sat in a corner in total darkness. Her legs were tied together and her hands were taped behind her back. The old door squeaked as it swung open. "Help me! I'm in here," she hollered, hoping that it was someone coming to save her. Hype came into clear view with a big smile on his face.

"Were you expecting someone else? Nobody will ever find you here."

"That's what you think."

"Everybody will think you're off with a man as usual."

"The police are looking for me right now."

"The call you made at the hotel. They just think it's another prank call."

"My rental is still there and besides, I didn't check out. Not to mention your blood in the room, you dummy. And other people will be looking for me when I don't show up to work."

"Who, Bling?" Hype laughed. "So you think he's going to leave his wife to come and save a bitch like you. So you're expecting Bling to be your hero. Stupid little bitch. He doesn't love you. You were just a bitch to all of us."

"This bitch played you for a fool!"

Hype went into the bag and took out some duct tape. He taped her mouth. He paced back and forth with the gun in his hand trying to come up with a quick plan.

"Everything was all good but you had to stir things up again. You couldn't accept the fact that all this was your fault and leave me alone. You just had to be the hero. Well, the joke is on you. Didn't you know the hero often dies in the end?"

Hype exited the abandoned building. His destination was to find Bling and this time when he would shoot he wouldn't miss his target. He knew he wouldn't be able to locate him on his own; he would have to call Rommel to help him out. He dialed the number and tried to keep his eyes on the road. His call went to voicemail after a few rings. "This is Mel, leave a message."

"Hit me back now." He pressed the end button. The light had turned red but his attention was set on dialing Rommel again. When he returned his attention to the road the car in front of him had stopped for the light. Hype slammed on his brakes to avoid a collision with the black Honda Accord and his phone fell. He beeped his horn two times to the tune of "fuck you," as if the driver had done something wrong. The light was now green and his phone started to ring at his feet. He tried to reach for it but his seat belt was preventing him. The cars behind him became impatient and beeped for him to go. He looked in his rearview mirror and stuck his middle finger up. He unbuckled his seat belt and reached for his phone. It was Rommel calling back. "We have work to do." He drove off through the yellow light, leaving a line of angry motorists behind.

"So what did you do with her?" Rommel asked.

"She's still breathing but I want you to help me locate Bling."

"What for?"

"I'm not leaving any stones unturned this time. I'm eliminating all of them. I'll be there in few minutes."

When Hype got to Rommel's house there was a suitcase on the floor. "Where the hell are you going? I just told you I need your help."

"Open the suitcase and stop running your mouth."

Hype unzipped the suitcase and his eyes widened. It was a collection of guns. "Oh, shit!"

"You can't go to war with a knife. Choose a winner."

"Where the hell did you get all these guns?"

"What do you mean where? All you need is money and you buy it from anywhere, even from the police."

"You're rolling deep!" Hype picked up a pump rifle and examined it.

Rommel took it from him. "You came to the machine shop and that is what you want?" Rommel gave him the Uzi.

"You're acting as if I'm going to fight war with Iraq." Hype put it back in the suitcase.

"A war is a war. Why not fight in style? When again are you going to have the chance to fire this." He showed him a Magnum.

"It's not that serious; this will do." He took the .45 pistol he had in his back that he had taken from Keisha.

"Remind me not to ask for your help in a real war," Rommel stated, shaking his head and zipping the suitcase. "Times like these you know who the real shottas are." Rommel put the suitcase under the bed.

"Stop all that talking and hurry up. We have work to do."

They circled the block looking for Bling. They even went to a few barber shops hoping to spot him. They went to the gym where he usually went for a workout but there was no sign of him. "I have to get something to eat. A burger will do me good right about now."

"We can't leave right now. I just have a feeling he's going to show up." They waited for almost an hour. Hype was about to drive off when a crisp black Lexus drove into the parking lot.

"Lay back!" Hype ordered, dropping back in his seat.

The car door opened and Bling stepped out, wearing basketball shorts and a white tee.

"Bingo!" Hype rubbed his hands together, getting anxious. "Let's get this bitch." He was ready to go after Bling.

"Hold on. There are too many people in the parking lot."

"Get out the car and go get him and stop acting like a pussy."

Rommel got out of the car and walked over to Bling, who was now searching in his car trunk. Rommel ran up to him, jamming the gun in his rib cage. "Take a walk with me, partner."

"Who the fuck are you?"

Rommel poked him deeper in his side and pushed him forward. They got to the car and Rommel opened the back door. "Get in, bitch." Bling hesitated and Rommel hit him with the gun over his head and blood flowed instantly. Bling got in the car and Rommel got in next to him.

"What the fuck do you want from me?" Bling wiped the blood from his face.

"I want your life, bitch," Hype stated while pointing the gun in his face. Bling swallowed hard. "How is that pretty wife of yours; is she ready for a real man?"

"You better not touch her!" Bling tried to get at Hype but before he could throw a blow Rommel hit him in the back of his head with the gun. Blood gushed out, turning the back of his white T-shirt red. He reached for the gun he religiously traveled with in his left sock, for he knew this day would come. But he refrained from using it just yet because if he made one wrong move he would be dead. Bling instinctively took his shirt off and rolled it into a ball, adding pressure to the back of his head to stop the bleeding. Bling relaxed his head on the seat because there was nothing he could do; but at the right moment Hype and Rommel would be dead.

Bling thought about his wife, suddenly feeling the guilt of never ending his relationship with Keisha even though he had promised her that he did. He had falling out of love with his wife and in love with Keisha.

"Where is she?" Bling asked but got no answer. Bling adjusted his body and look at Hype with rage in his eyes. "If you hurt her I will—"

Before he could finish his sentence Rommel had the gun at his head. "You will do what?"

Bling calmed his anger and looked out the window and noticed he was heading north on I-95. "Where are you taking me?"

"Relax and enjoy the ride." Hype dashed into the center lane to get from behind a car that was moving too slow, but quickly jammed on his brakes when another car switched into the same lane as him, causing Bling's body to lunge forward. Hype switched to the right lane, cutting off a white Camry, then accelerated on the gas pedal.

Thirty minutes into the ride they exited and got on the Van Wyck Expressway, then onto the Jackie Robinson Parkway. Rommel put a paper bag over Bling's head to prevent him from seeing their location. They pulled up at their destination and two crackheads sitting outside ran when they saw Hype exiting the car. It was still bright outside but the police rarely drove on these streets.

They entered through the back door and had to maneuver their way past high grass that hadn't been mowed in years. They pushed Bling inside with the bag still over his head. Rommel removed the bag from Bling's head and

Keisha's eyes bulged in disbelief. She wiggled her body, trying to set herself free. Hype pushed Bling toward her. "Is he supposed to be your knight in shining armor?"

Bling ran to her. He removed the tape from her mouth. "Are you okay!" he asked her.

Hype was laughing at the sight of Keisha and Bling together. Rommel was standing guard over them. "Is he supposed to be your hero? I brought him to you. You said he was going to save you, right? Let me see him try."

Bling wanted to pull his gun from his sock but he knew Hype wouldn't hesitate to shoot him or Keisha. Hype got close to Bling and pointed the gun to his forehead. "I can promise you that I won't miss my target this time." Hype knocked Bling on his head with the gun and he fell to the floor.

"Nooooo!" Keisha screamed but Hype laughed at her.

"Isn't he supposed to be your hero? What a shame he can't even save himself."

"You are going to pay for this!" Keisha tried to free herself.

"Just in case you didn't notice, I am untouchable. The police couldn't find me and your boyfriend couldn't take me down. I am king! You could have been my queen, my empress, but you like the lifestyle of a bitch and a bitch can't wear the crown. You aren't royal; you are nothing but a bitch for hire. Oh, by the way, didn't your uncle hire you as a hooker to do his dirty work?"

"Don't you dare speak his name. You are a monster who doesn't deserve to live. You are a weak person who hides behind a gun to do your dirty work. You aren't man enough just like you weren't man enough for me."

Hype put the tape back over her mouth. "Duct tape his hands," he ordered Rommel to duct tape Bling. Keisha tried to speak but the tape captured every word that tried to escape.

"I have to get rid of you and your little friend and I have the perfect plan. First I'm going to cut him into little pieces and turn him into fish food. Then I'm going to sell you to the highest bidder and then take the money and pay my boat connection to take me away from here. Come on, Rommel, let's go!" He walked off to the door. "Don't move a muscle." Hype laughed a devilish laugh and exited the house.

Keisha tried desperately to free herself but her skin burned as she fought with the tape. Her eyes watered as the pain worsened. She let out a loud cry but the tape caught the sound. She had rubbed the skin from her wrist. After several minutes of agonizing pain the tape had loosened enough for her to painfully remove one of her hands. She took the tape off her mouth then rushed to Bling and freed him too. "Bling can you hear me?" She shook his body.

"Mmmhh." Bling turned his head and moaned in agony.

"Can you hear me? Get up! We have to get out of here!" She was now crying because Bling was incoherent and her wrist was burning like it was on fire. She tried to pick him up but he was much too heavy for her to carry. She tried to pull him by his arm but she only dragged him about a couple of feet before she gave up. With tears rolling down her face she begged and pleaded for him to get up. "You have to get up! I can't carry you! You have to get up!" She wiped her tears and tried to think of a plan to get out of there before Hype returned. She tried picking him up again but it wasn't progressive.

"I have to go. I have to leave but I'll be back. I have to go get help. I promise I'll be back." She ran outside but she was surrounded by abandoned houses on both sides. She ran a few blocks but she couldn't go as fast as she would have liked because she was weak from not eating.

She finally came upon a few houses that were occupied by residents. The first door she knocked on no one came to her rescue. She knocked on a few more doors but to no avail. She was getting restless when she saw a house with a car in the driveway. She gathered all the energy she had left in her body and ran to the house.

She knocked the door and rang the bell and a man opened the door. "Please, sir. You have to help me. Call the police." The man closed the door in her face. She banged on the door again. "Please, please, you have to help me." Tears ran down her face but she knew she had to keep going. She could barely walk but she made it to another house. She knocked on the door but no one came. All her energy was now gone. She could barely put one foot in front of the other. There was a stop sign in front of her. She reached for it, holding on for support, but her arms gave out. She fell to the ground and everything was spinning around her. She closed her eyes and drifted off into darkness.

Chapter 27

Keisha woke up to the sound of voices. She looked through blurry vision and saw alligator shoes and another set of feet wearing shiny red pimp shoes. She didn't recognize where she was. It wasn't the same place she was before. She felt two strong arms bringing her to her feet. Two black guys and one Spanish guy stood in front of her dressed like pimps.

"Still interested to buy this bitch?" the man behind her holding her up asked. "I know she is a little dirty but all she needs is a little cleaning up." One of the pimps was holding a water bottle and he tossed it on her face. She took a deep breath as if she was drowning. "See she is just fine. With some makeup you could make back triple the price I'm going charge for her." The men nodded their heads as if sealing a deal.

"How much?" the Spanish man asked.

"Give me five thousand and she is all yours."

Keisha started to kick and scream. She was going to be sold to the highest bidder. "I'll give you six," the man wearing the alligator shoes said, taking out his wallet.

"What about you, red shoe?" the man holding her asked.

The man shook his head. "The price is too high." He walked out of the room.

"Well, she's sold to you then, pimp daddy in the gator shoes."

There was a knock on the door as Gator Shoes was counting out his money and put it on the table. The big-bellied sweaty man released Keisha to Gator Shoes. "Who is it?" he responded to the knock as he exited the room, closing the door behind him. "I think I want to sample you before I release you to the vultures at my whorehouse." Gator Shoes smiled, showing his gold teeth as he planted a kiss in the nape of Keisha's neck.

"So where is the girl?" Keisha heard the big-bellied sweaty man ask whoever it was he was speaking to. It was hard to hear what the other person was saying but Big Belly was so loud everyone could hear his sweaty ass. "I'll take her off your hands if the price is right."

Gator Shoes opened the door with his left hand while his right hand held Keisha around her waist with a tight grip. Keisha knew that what she was about to get was worse than being tied up in that abandoned house. At least she would have still been with Bling. Gator Shoes escorted Keisha out the room and stepped toward the door. Keisha saw the red exit sign and she went wild like a raging bull. "Help! Somebody help me!" Gator Shoes couldn't contain her. She got away from his grip and ran in the opposite direction. The fat sweaty bastard came around the corner and Keisha wasn't surprised to see who was with him. Regardless if she wanted to stop running her legs froze when she saw Hype because for sure her life was now over. Gator Shoes ran up and grabbed her and she didn't struggle or fight back; everything was going wrong. She was caught in a tangled web with no way out. Anyway you looked at it she was fucked.

"What the fuck!" were the words that came from Hype's mouth.

"She is a hot one but she's all mine. Bought and paid for," Gator replied.

"Can your girl top that?" Sweaty Man asked. Gator took a few steps to the door, wanting to go home with his new purchase, but Hype blocked him from leaving.

"You're not going anywhere!" Hype stated with words of war.

Gator Shoes paused. "What you doing, young buck?"

"This is my bitch. You're not going anywhere with her."

"Hold your horses, young buck. Like the man said, she is bought and paid for." Sweaty Man tried to defuse the situation.

"And like I said this is my bitch. He isn't going nowhere with her." Hype took his gun out of his waist.

"What the fuck are you doing?" Sweaty Man was coughing from the cigar he was smoking.

"I picked this bitch up off the side off the road. So she belongs to me and like I said, she's sold."

"She wasn't yours to sell because she belongs to me."

"I just made a six pack off this bitch and you expect me to give it back?" Sweaty Man chuckled, causing himself to cough uncontrollable.

"Let go of her!" Hype ordered, pointing the gun at Gator Shoes, and he complied. Keisha took a few steps backward but Sweaty Man grabbed on to her.

"It's not that easy, young buck. Her price just went up."

"Release her or he's dead," Hype threatened.

"You wouldn't do that, young buck. It's not wise to mix business with pleasure."

"It's all business to me." Bang! The gun went off and Gator Shoes was on the floor.

"Ahhh!" Keisha screamed, covering her ears.

"You don't have to refund him but you will refund this bitch." Hype was walking closer to him and Sweaty Man was stepping backward.

"You know that's not how it works, young buck. Nothing in this world is for free. Money makes this world go around."

"And you are fucking with my money." Hype fired a shot and it connected with Sweaty Man's shoulder. His arm went limp and Keisha fell to the ground.

Sweaty Man ran for cover. "Bitch, you are more trouble than you're worth." He grabbed Keisha by the arm, pulling her to the door.

"Get off me!" Keisha was kicking and screaming. He dress rode up on her ass, exposing her panties. She was looking like a dirty crackhead whore. Just days ago she was a woman in a business suit. If anyone had told her that she would be kidnapped, raped, bought, and sold she would have told them to go seek mental help. But here she was living what seemed to be a nightmare and couldn't wake up. The front door of the building open and a bright light appeared. Keisha was hoping that she had died and gone to heaven. But that wasn't the case when shots were flying past her.

"Ahhh," Keisha screamed, covering her ears as Hype ran for cover. She was in the middle of a shootout. With each shot fired she reacted with an even louder scream. In a panic Keisha got up and tried to run but a bullet pierced her in the back.

Bling came into clear view as she fell to the floor. Hype had shot her. He wanted to get rid of her and the bullet from his gun did the job. The gun fire had stopped giving her a moment of silence. Hype took the moment to make his escape. But Bling fired at him as he made his exit. Bling ran after him and noticed a trail of blood leading him to Hype. He was trying to put the key in the ignition of the car but the keys fell out of his shaking hand. He bent to pick up the keys and he raised his head to the warmth of Bling's gun. "Game over, fool!" Bling squeezed his trigger and Hype's head fell on the steering wheel and the horn stayed on as he emptied his gun and his blood splattered all over the car.

Bling rushed back to Keisha and laid her head in his lap. "You're going to be okay. You are going to be okay." Keisha nodded her head and closed her eyes. Everything was now a blur to Keisha. Her focus was gone. "Wake up, Wake up! Don't die on me." Bling was shaking her body. "Don't die on me! You can't die! I love you." Keisha heard the words but she was drifting further into unconsciousness but managed to say a prayer.

"Dear God, please spare my life so I can right my wrongs." Then came darkness. Bling held her lifeless body pleading with her to come back.

"Put your hands up! Put your hands up!" the police ordered but Bling held on to Keisha without acknowledging their presence. "Put your hands up!" the police ordered. But still he didn't comply. A cop slowly crept up from behind, putting him into a chokehold and another quickly put him in cuffs. "Call the medics!" the officer who had him in a chokehold yelled. "You are under arrest. Anything you say can and will be held against you . . ."

Notes